CREEPIN': A NEW ORLEANS LOVE STORY

BY: CHENELL PARKER

OTHER TITLES BY ME INCLUDE:

HER SO CALLED HUSBAND PARTS 1-3

YOU'RE MY LITTLE SECRET PARTS 1-3

WHAT YOU WON'T DO FOR LOVE

STAY CONNECTED WITH ME:

amazon.com/author/chenellparker

https://twitter.com/cocochenell504

https://www.goodreads.com/author/show/8407468.Chen
ell_Parker

Also under Chenell Parker or Author Chenell Parker on
Facebook

Chapter 1

"Hold my purse," Lamia instructed her best friend, Brandis, as they walked down the hallway of their school. She'd already taken off her earrings and chain and dropped them inside of her Gucci hobo bag. It was the last day of Lamia's junior year and she'd just gotten the last of her exam grades back. She was officially a senior and she was ready to celebrate the start of her summer. Her excitement was short lived when she saw two of her enemies headed in her direction. Sariah and Shania were sisters who hated Lamia with a passion. It was crazy because they really didn't know each other very well. They were fighting a battle for their auntie because she was too old to do it on her own.

The sisters were eighteen and nineteen years old, but had never made it out of the eleventh grade. Thanks to them, Lamia was always getting suspended because she was always getting into a fight. Lamia regretted staying for the entire day, but she had some last minute things that she had to take care of. The only reason why she'd come to school in the first place was to get her final grades and last report card. After being on suspension for most of the year, she was surprised that she passed at all. At only seventeen years old, Lamia Walker was considered to be one of the most popular females at her high school. She was also considered to be the hottest. With dark brown flawless skin and a Coke bottle shape, she was often compared to Taylour Paige from the TV show *Hit the Floor*, but she didn't see the resemblance.

"Hell no, if you fight I'm fighting too," Brandis replied as she removed her earrings as well. "Hold our stuff," Brandis said while handing over her and Lamia's handbags to Eric, one of her former classmates.

She knew that Lamia could handle herself well, but there was no way that she was letting them jump her girl. A few people stopped what they were doing and watched the group of girls because they already knew what was about to take place. This was nothing new to see Lamia and Brandis fighting with one, or both of the sisters at any given time. Mia always wondered why they started with her when she'd already whipped both of their asses on several occasions. They still didn't get the hint, but she had no problem doing it again.

"You have a problem with our auntie Lamia?" Shania asked. She was the loudest one of the two sisters and she always liked to cause a scene. "I mean, you playing on her phone and shit so there must be a problem."

"Bitch, your auntie is damn near thirty years old and still playing these lil' childish ass games. You know damn well I'm not playing on that hoe's phone, but she seems to know my number by memory. Twenty-eight years old and still trying to fight over a nigga," Lamia yelled.

"That's just it though, Tank is her man so she don't have to fight you over him," Shania replied.

"Okay, so if he's her man then what's the problem? Y'all always come at me for what reason?" Lamia asked angrily.

"The problem is you being disrespectful. You know they're together so why would you come around her house in his car? Why call his phone when you know he's with her?" Shania growled while her sister continued to remain silent.

"Well tell your auntie to ask her man why he gives me the keys to his car. And if he's at her house why does he answer the phone when I call? If you ask me, that nigga is the one that's being disrespectful. I don't owe your auntie shit and Tank ain't my man," Lamia argued.

"Well you need to stop acting like it," Sariah said, finally finding her voice.

"Nah, that nigga needs to stop acting like it," Brandis spoke up for her girl.

"Man, what's up? I have somewhere to be and I don't have time for all this talking," Lamia added.

"It's whatever," Shania answered while dropping her bag to the floor. Before she even looked up Lamia pounced on her and Brandis did the same to her sister. Since the sisters were caught off guard, their opponents were quickly able to get the best of them. Thankfully for them, the fight didn't last long and security was rushing to break it up. Brandis grabbed their bags from Eric right before she was escorted out of the building right behind her friend.

"Tell your auntie about that beat down, bitch," Lamia yelled while being carried away from the brawl.

"Girl, come on here and go home," one of the security guards said while making sure Lamia got out of the building safely. "I keep telling you that you are too pretty to be out here fighting all the time."

"You act like I come here to fight. I come to school and mind my business, but somebody always has something to say to me," Lamia shouted.

"I know Mia, but you have to learn to ignore that sometimes. That ain't nothing but jealousy," he replied. "Y'all start walking home. I'll keep them here for a while to make sure y'all don't start up again."

Lamia wanted to protest, but it was pointless at the moment. She got her bag from Brandis and put her jewelry back on, while they made the five-block walk to their homes. The Courtyard Apartments, where they resided, used to be the projects until the city got a grant and remodeled them. They now consisted of two, three and four-bedroom apartments with ceramic tile and state of

7

the art appliances. It was still considered the projects to Lamia, but everybody now called it The Court. The same people still lived back there, but now they had a set of strict rules to follow, or risk being evicted. Brandis was not only Lamia's best friend, she was also her neighbor.

"I guess you and Tank are about to have it out now," Brandis commented while they were walking.

"Fuck Tank!" Lamia spat angrily. "I knew what it was when I got with that nigga. I don't expect anything to be different now."

"But that's your fault Mia. It's not like he don't want to be with you. You're the one who wants to keep y'all relationship a secret," Brandis reminded her.

"Yeah, but he knows why."

"I guess, but are you going by Von's this weekend?" Brandis asked changing the subject.

"Girl yes, you know I look forward to my weekends. I need to get away from The Court for a few days," Lamia sighed.

Trevon or Von was Lamia's Godfather. He was her father's best friend and the only consistent person in her life. He treated her and his other Godchild, Rainey, like they were his very own. His house had been their home every weekend for years. Lamia's father, Lamar, Rainey's father,

Reynard, and Von had been best friends since they were in elementary school. They got money together and you rarely saw one without the other. Von christened both of his best friends' daughters and nothing was too good for his girls. When Von got locked up and did eight years in prison, Lamar and Reynard took care of his one and only son, Trevon Jr., until he was released. He had three brothers, but his friends stepped up to the plate on his behalf. When Von came home, he decided that hustling was no longer what he wanted to do. Tre was only two when he got locked up and he'd already missed out on eight years of his life. Then to make matters worse, he had to leave Tre with his mother, who wasn't fit to care for a dog in his opinion.

Tre's mother, Terri, was unfit in every sense of the word. Not only was she a horrible mother to Tre, but she had the nerve to have two more kids after him. Von hustled long enough to open up a few legal businesses before he decided that he was done. Over the course of three years, he'd acquired several lucrative businesses throughout New Orleans and the surrounding areas. Aside from a few rental properties, he had two barbershops, a car wash and a recording studio that he rented out by the day. He'd recently obtained partnership into a successful gym, and the money was rolling in. The recording studio alone made enough to pay his bills for the month, so he was satisfied. He also made sure that Tre never had to work a day in his life if he didn't want to. He acquired just as much property for his son as he'd gotten for himself and he, too, was set. Von never imagined that he could live just as good off of legal money, so selling drugs was a thing of the past for him.

Sadly, his best friends weren't on the same page as him. Hustling was all that they knew, so they continued to make money without him. Things really went downhill from there. Four years after Von was released from prison, Reynard was killed in a drug deal gone wrong. Some youngsters asked to buy something from him, but they robbed and killed him instead. Von was devastated, but not more than Lamar. When Von went to jail, Lamar and Reynard got very close and he was taking his friend's death hard. He was having a hard time coping, so he turned to drugs to take the pain away. It started with him snorting a few lines of coke until he had a heroin addiction that was hard to break. Von almost lost his mind over everything that had happened, but he never turned his back on his friend. When Lamar lost his house, Von furnished one of his rental properties and made sure that he always had a roof over his head. He picked up his clothes once a week and made sure they were always clean. Lamar was on drugs, but he was always neat, clean and well fed, thanks to his best friend. Aside from the obvious weight loss, it was hard to even tell. His name still rang bells in the projects right along with Von's.

"Ask Von if I can come over and swim tomorrow," Brandis said pulling Lamia away from her thoughts.

"You know he won't mind. They don't even use that pool unless we're over there," Lamia replied.

"I don't have to ask if he's grilling. That's his every weekend routine."

"Yep, but me and Rainey can pick you up tomorrow whenever you're ready to come over," Lamia offered.

"No thanks, I'll get a ride or I'll catch the bus," Brandis frowned.

"I don't know why you don't like my sister."

"God sister," Brandis corrected. "And I don't like her because she's always looking down on everybody. I'm happy that her mama's new husband was able to move them out of the projects, but everybody is not as fortunate. A year ago, she was in the same situation that we're in now. She got a car and a bigger house and now she can't stand the projects no more."

Lamia understood what her friend was saying, but she ignored Rainey's new attitude. Her mama got married two years ago to a welder, and they'd purchased a huge house not too far from where Von lived. When they purchased Rainey a Maxima a few months ago, her entire attitude changed. All of a sudden, she hated coming to the same projects that she used to live in not too long ago. Everything was cheap and ghetto to her now.

11

She still went to the same school, but she ran with a whole new group of girls. All of them had cars, but that was about the only thing that they had in common. She really looked down on Brandis because she didn't dress in labels like most girls her age. She came from a single parent home and it just wasn't in their budget. It never bothered Mia because she made sure her girl was together before they went anywhere.

"Girl, you know you don't have to catch the bus. I'll ask Von or Tre to pick you up. Maybe you can spend the night if it's okay with your mama."

"You know she be acting stupid sometimes, but I'll see. Maybe her boyfriend will give her some and she'll be in a good mood," Brandis laughed.

"I'll talk to you later. Just let me know so I can tell Von," Lamia said before walking into her apartment. Brandis lived in the building right next to hers so she kept going.

"Hey Mia," her little sister Anika spoke when Mia walked through the front door. She was the youngest of the six of them and she was bad as hell. At only eight years old, Anika had a mouth that was worse than some grown women. Their mother only laughed when she cursed, but Lamia would slap her in the mouth.

"Hey, where is Moonie?" Lamia asked referring to their mother.

"She's in the room with her stupid boyfriend," Anika responded.

Aside from Anika, Lamia had three brothers and one other sister. Her oldest brother, Jabari, didn't live with them and he didn't come to visit very often. He lived with his girlfriend, so Mia and the other kids went to visit them instead. He and Moonie didn't get along, so he stayed his distance. Moonie was the true definition of a baby having babies and it showed. At only thirty-five years old, Moonie had Jabari when she was fifteen. By the time she made eighteen, Jabari was three years old and she'd already given birth to Lamia. Just about every man she met became her baby daddy. She had four already and she wasn't with any of them. Two of them helped out financially and that was all that Moonie cared about. She'd never had a job that Mia could remember, but their four-bedroom apartment was laid from top to bottom. It was so nice that the complex used their house as the apartment to show to potential new renters, and it was also featured in their brochure. All of her kids had the latest gear and her cabinets were always overflowing with food. She wasn't a bad person, but she didn't have a maternal bone in her body. She went out damn near every night and she seemed more like her children's friend than their mother. Jabari used to be okay with it until she started messing with one of his best friends. He didn't care that she dated younger men, but his friend should have never been one of them.

"Where is everybody else?" Lamia asked.

"They're outside, but Moonie punished me," Anika pouted.

"Why are you punished? What did you do?"

"Nothing, but the lady downstairs told Moonie that I cursed her out. Jabari said he coming to get me tonight though."

Lamia laughed because she knew that whatever the neighbors said about her little sister was probably true. Mia took the keys out of her purse and opened her bedroom door. Her little brothers and sisters were too damn bad to leave it unlocked. Besides Moonie, she was the only one who had her own room. Just like the rest of the house, her room was decked out with the latest furniture and decorations. There were two boys and two girls to the other two bedrooms, with two bathrooms to share among them all. After opening her walk-in closet, Mia thumbed through the hundreds of outfits, trying to decide on what she was going to take with her. She noticed that a few new items had been added to her collection letting her know that her mother had been shopping recently. Moonie was all about appearances, so she and her kids had more clothes than they actually needed. She had lots of enemies, so she had to make sure that she and her kids were always on point. There was no way in hell that Moonie wasn't giving her haters something to talk about.

"Mia," Moonie yelled while banging on her bedroom door. Lamia rolled her eyes to the ceiling while walking to the door to let her mother in.

14

"What Moonie?" she asked while walking back to her closet.

"Are you going by Von and Tre's this weekend?" she asked taking a seat on her daughter's bed.

"Yep, so I can't babysit your kids for you," Mia snapped before the question was even asked.

"It's cool; they're going by Jabari's until tomorrow anyway. He's taking them to a party or something," Moonie replied. She got up and looked out of Mia's bedroom window giving Mia a chance to really study her. After having six kids, Moonie was still the shit. She had a very pretty face and a shape that still had men paying all of her bills. Her stomach wasn't flat, but it wasn't so big that her clothes couldn't conceal it. She wore her hair short and she never kept it the same color for more than a few months at a time. Moonie had a small waist and an ass so huge that it almost looked like it was detached from her body. Everybody said that Lamia got her looks and shape from her mother and in her opinion, that was a very good compliment.

"You paid my phone bill?" Lamia asked her.

"Baby girl, every bill in here is paid up for this month and the next. I hope you don't think these nigga be smiling in my face for nothing. I got you some stuff from the mall earlier too," Moonie replied.

"I saw that," Mia replied. "I hope you didn't let anybody in my room."

"You know I wouldn't let anybody in here. I put it up myself." Aside from her, Moonie was the only other person with a key to her bedroom.

"And don't let Dalvin be having his friends all up in here and shit. He gon' have us getting put out while he be living good by his mama's. You already know these people don't play that."

Dalvin was one of Moonie's boyfriends who spent some nights at their house. He was only twenty-nine years old, but he took care of Moonie like money grew on trees. Lamia thought he was stupid because Moonie was always playing him to the left. She wouldn't even answer the phone for him sometimes when she wanted to have somebody else at the house. He didn't have a key, but he paid the bills faithfully every month like his name was on the lease. When Moonie wanted a new truck, he hustled day and night until he was able to get it for her without having to pay a note on it. People were always telling him that he was being played, but he wasn't trying to hear it.

"I know Mia, damn. That only happened one time. We're going out tonight anyway. When I come back in here, I'm going straight to bed," Moonie replied.

"Alright, well I'm about to call Rainey to pick me up."

"Okay, tell Von that I said hey," Moonie said as she got up and walked away.

Chapter 2

"What took you so long?" Rainey fussed when Mia got into her car. "You know I hate sitting out here too long."

"Girl, stop acting like you didn't grow up back here. It's not even that serious," Lamia argued. "You're the one who waited until it got dark to come get me."

"And who scratched up your face like that?" Rainey questioned.

"I had a fight at school earlier. Don't even ask with who because you already know. The last day of school and those bitches wanted to fight. I didn't even notice the shit until I looked in the mirror earlier."

"They're fighting over Tank like he's their man. That's my boy and all, but you need to leave his ass alone. Either that or let people know that y'all are together. I really don't see what the problem is."

"I wish everybody would just leave it alone. If we're cool with the way things are then everybody else should be cool with it too," Lamia hissed.

"But he's not cool with it. You get mad when he's with other people, but you don't want to be with him."

"It's not that I don't want to be with him, it's just complicated. You of all peopled should know that."

"Yeah okay, just don't get mad when he does him," Rainey spat.

She and Lamia traveled the rest of the way to Vons's house in silence. Lamia understood what everybody was saying, but things weren't that simple to her. She didn't want to disappoint anyone and exposing her relationship with Tank was sure to do that.

"I hope Von cooked, I'm starving," Rainey said when they pulled into their Godfather's driveway.

"You know he did. That's all he does is cook," Lamia said laughing. "I see that bitch, Cheryl is already here."

"Leave that lady alone Mia. I don't know what you have against her."

"I don't have anything against her, but she doesn't like me for whatever reason. She's nice to you and Tre, but she always gives me the side eye. She's even nice to Brandis when she comes over here. I don't know what her problem is with me," Mia shrugged.

"You better not tell that to Von. He'll probably leave her alone for messing with his favorite Godchild," Rainey replied sarcastically.

"Don't even start with your shit. He treats both of us the same, so I don't know why you always say that."

"Lamia please, now I won't lie and say that he's not good to both of us, but he clearly favors you more than me," Rainey responded. Mia didn't say anything because what her God sister said was true. She knew that she had a special place in Von's heart. Her father was on drugs and her mother was a street runner. Von felt like she had it harder than Rainey, so he catered to her just a little bit more.

"Hey my babies," Von smiled when the girls walked into the kitchen. He was just taking some stuffed bell peppers out of the oven while he had the cooking oil getting hot to fry some fish. Cheryl sat at the kitchen table playing on her phone, while Tre sat at the island with a Heineken in front of him.

"Hey y'all," Lamia and Rainey spoke in unison. They went down the hall to put their bags away before rejoining everyone in the kitchen.

"Who did your hair Rainey? It's pretty," Cheryl said while running her fingers through Rainey's bone-straight sew-in. She never did acknowledge Mia, but that was fine with her.

"It's a shop uptown. They're high, but it's well worth it," Rainey bragged. "I got tired of getting my hair done in people's kitchens in the projects. All they do is gossip."

"I know that's right," Cheryl co-signed. "I told my daughter about letting them project hood rats get in her head, but she won't listen. She likes being in the midst of all of that mess and foolishness for some reason."

Lamia could have been offended, but she let their comments slide just like she always did. Cheryl was always making slick remarks about the projects and Rainey always fell right into her trap.

"Y'all talking that shit, but some of them projects chicks do hair better than those high-priced shops that y'all go to," Von chimed in. He knew that they were throwing slugs at Mia, but she always handled herself well in any situation.

"You need some help Von?" Mia offered ignoring the negative comments.

"Yeah, get the fish fry for me Mimi," he replied, calling her by the nickname he had given her when she was a baby. Lamia looked in the refrigerator and cabinets, but came up empty. Once she searched the pantry closet, she realized that Von was out of what he needed.

"You don't have any more fish fry Von. You want me to go to the store?" she offered.

"Shit," Von cursed. "No, but turn that stove off for me. I need to get some more beer anyway and they won't sell it to you. I'll fry the fish when I come back. Y'all want something?"

"I'm coming with you," Cheryl replied while everybody else declined.

"You good Mimi?" Von asked while looking over at her. Before she could respond, he grabbed her face and inspected it closely. "What the hell happened to your face? Who scratched you up like that?"

"I had a fight at school today," she answered while giving Tre the screw face.

"I don't know why you won't let me put you in a private school. This is your last year and you don't need to be doing all that fighting," Von fussed.

"You should Mia; I'm going to St. Mary's Academy next year and I can't wait," Rainey butted in.

"That's all on you, but I don't want to go to a private school. I've been at Landry since I was in the ninth grade and all of my friends are there. I'm not scared and I'm not running from nobody. They're trying to fight me over a nigga that I don't even want," Mia said, causing Tre to snap his head around in her direction.

"They gon' make me pay somebody to come back there and beat their lil' stupid asses down," Von fumed as he grabbed his keys and left.

As soon as the door closed, Tre was in Mia's face going off. "So you don't want me now Mia?" he asked angrily.

"Nigga fuck you," Lamia spat as she tried to walk past him.

"Can we please have one weekend without y'all two getting into it?" Rainey begged.

"I'm good, but Tank seems to be the one with the problem," Mia answered.

"Don't call me that shit man," Tre yelled.

"Why can't I call you Tank? That's what everybody else calls you," Mia taunted.

"Well you're not everybody else, so don't call me that. Come here and let me talk to you," Tre said while pulling her down the hall to the bedroom.

"Stop pulling on me boy. We could have talked right in the kitchen," Mia fussed.

"Let me see your face," he instructed once they were alone.

"Nah nigga, don't worry about my face. You better get your bitch in check because I'm tired of playing these games with her old ass. How does she send her nieces at me and those scary bitches can't even fight?"

"But why you mad with me though? This is what you wanted right? You were the one who said don't tell nobody that we mess around."

"And you know why I said that. You know Von would have a fit if he knew what was going on with us. We damn near grew up in the same house Tre."

"That's bullshit Mia. I'm twenty-one years old and I've been in and out of jail since I was sixteen. I barely saw you when you came over here because I was hardly here myself. You act like we're on some incest shit or something. We're not even related so I don't see what the problem is."

"I know that, but you know your daddy still won't approve of us being together. I feel bad enough when he introduces us to people as brother and sister."

"He's your Godfather Mia, of course he's going to feel like that. But I'm too old to be doing this secret lovers creepin' shit. We've been doing this for over a year now and it's getting old. You need to make up your mind about what you really want because this is childish."

"Maybe it's because I'm a child," Mia pointed out.

"Girl you ain't no damn child. You're about to be eighteen years old in a few months. Besides, you don't act like a child when you be twerking that ass in the bedroom," Tre smirked. "Let me get some right quick before Von comes back."

"Hell no, I'm not fucking with you like that no more. You can keep Paige with her old worn out dusty ass."

"So what, you jealous now?" Tre asked while kissing her on the neck.

"Jealous?" Mia roared. "Nigga you must be crazy. You must not know how many niggas be checking for my fine ass. Hell, even some of your friends be trying to get at me."

"Who?" Tre yelled with a frown covering his handsome face. "Which one of my friends be flirting with you?"

"Shit, nigga take your pick. But it's all good if you want to do you. Just don't get mad when I do me. You might have been the first one to hit it, but that don't mean that you'll be the last one to get it."

"Fuck with me if you want to. Please, I'm begging you to play with me. I guarantee you that Von and everybody else in New Orleans gon' know what's up," he swore.

"Oh, so I'm supposed to sit back and be cool while you fuck with other people. You got me messed up for real."

"Again, this is all on you. These are your rules that I'm playing by. I'm dancing to your music, so don't get mad with me. When we first starting messing around I told you that I wanted to be with you. I left everybody else alone just to make it happen. You were the one who didn't want Von to find out."

Lamia didn't respond because Tre was right. She really did love him, but she knew that Von wouldn't approve of them being together. Von was like a father to her and she couldn't imagine being the one to disappoint him. Things with her and Tre should have never gone that far, but it was too late since both of their feelings were involved. Before Tre came home last year, he and Mia would see each other off and on every now and then, but he was always on the go. Things were different this time around. Before, Mia was a flat-chested, cute girl with a pencil thin body and long hair. In only a year's time, she'd blossomed into a beautiful young woman with a nice shape and a style of her own. All that brother and sister talk went out the window for Tre. He finally saw Lamia as more than just his God sister and he let her know. At first, she was scared to deal with him on that level, but things changed after a while. He used to sneak in the spare bedroom where she slept and they would only touch and kiss. After a few months of that, Mia finally let him take her virginity. Once Tre got a taste of her virgin goodies he wanted her all to himself, but Mia wasn't ready. She agreed to keep dealing with him, but only if they could keep it between the two of them. Tre was okay with it at first, but that quickly got old to him. He wanted to be with her and he didn't care how anybody felt about it. When he expressed his feelings to Mia, she flipped out and decided that it was best for them to just end it. Tre wasn't trying to hear that, so he once again played by her rules. Only this time, he had some rules of his own. He let Lamia know that until she was ready to announce their relationship to the world, he was free to do whatever he wanted. Technically, he was still single since she refused to commit. He'd even ended things with Paige just to be with her. After things didn't work out like he wanted them to with Mia, he started kicking it with his ex-girlfriend again. Paige was seven years older than Tre and they'd been off and on since he was sixteen years old. Von couldn't stand her because she already had three kids when she and Tre met. He felt that she was too old for his son and she already had a family. Paige was Tre's first sex partner, so he thought he was in love with her until he started messing with Mia.

"Von just pulled up," Rainey yelled while knocking on the bedroom door. Both Lamia and Tre jumped up and headed back to the kitchen.

"Leave the door unlocked so I can come back once everybody goes to sleep," Tre told Mia while giving her a peck on the lips. He hated the situation that they were in, but he wasn't ready to leave it alone just yet.

***

"Nigga you a fucking lie!" Paige yelled to Tre. He was sitting there playing dumb and it was pissing her off. "You're car wasn't at the shop, you let that bitch drive it while you were on your bike. My nieces saw her and her friends at the mall."

"Girl get out of my damn face before you make me lose my game," he said in an uncaring tone. He was more focused on the video game than their conversation.

"She's lucky I didn't tell them to whip her ass again."

"I don't know what your nieces have been telling you, but they ain't been winning no fights over that way," he laughed.

"You think that shit is funny? You ain't nothing but a fucking pedophile messing with that young ass girl."

"Girl I know you didn't just say that shit. You were fucking me before I was even old enough to vote. And I keep telling you that I don't mess with that damn girl like that. All y'all muthafuckas on the outside looking in and don't know what's going on."

"Why do you keep lying? Y'all be trying to play that shit off, but I'm not stupid. Every time you get a new pair of shoes, she gets the same kind at the same time, so I know you're buying them for her too. She's always in your car and I never see you on the weekends because that's the time you spend with her."

"You don't see me on the weekends because I be busy. I have rental properties and businesses that require my full attention. I don't have time to be up under your ass all day."

"But you be all up under Mia though. You don't have to lie Tre," Paige teased just to make him mad.

"Don't call me that shit," he hissed.

"Why can't I call you Tre? That's what Lamia calls you right?"

"Don't worry about what she calls me. You been calling me Tank so don't try to switch it up now."

"I just don't understand you Trevon," Paige said getting serious. "I have a house, but you continue to live with your daddy. We've been together for five years now and you still won't commit. We were good before, but what am I doing so wrong now?"

"We've been together for five years, but you would have had a two-year-old child by somebody else if you wouldn't have gotten rid of it. And I used to live here until you decided that you didn't want me here anymore. That was your doing, not mine," he reminded her.

During one of his many visits to jail, Paige must have gotten tired of waiting for him. In just a matter of months, she'd moved somebody else into her apartment and went on with her life like it was nothing. She even had one of her brothers drop his clothes and the rest of his belongings off to Von's house. When Tre came home she was already pregnant by the other dude, but she decided that she wanted to make things work with him instead. She had an abortion and sent the other man on his way. Tre was all for it at first until the reality of the situation hit him. Paige had basically turned her back on him and he couldn't just forget about that. Once he started kicking it with Mia not too long after, it was a wrap for the two of them. He spent some nights over there when he felt like it, but he never did move back in like she wanted him to. In his mind, it was just something to do until Mia came to her senses and stopped being scared.

"I wish you would stop trying to punish me for my past mistakes. I've apologized a million times for that, but I can't take it back. As many times as you've cheated and dogged me out, you should be able to forgive and forget," Paige complained.

"All is forgiven and forgotten. That still doesn't mean that I have to be up under you all day though. And living with my pops is by choice. It's not like I can't afford my own place if I want one."

"Well you need to make that happen. I can't even see you if you don't come over here. You know I'm not welcomed in his house since he can't stand me. I really don't know why because I've never done anything to him," she pouted.

"Maybe it's because you were a twenty-three-year-old woman sleeping with his sixteen-year-old son," Tre laughed.

"I don't see what's so funny. It's no different than you sleeping with Lamia. I guess he gave y'all the green light since he loves her so much," Paige snapped.

"You can't go five minutes without bringing her up, huh? That damn girl don't even worry about you like that."

"Fuck her!" Paige yelled. "She's a hoe just like her mama. The apple really didn't fall far from the tree."

"Now why you gotta bring Moonie up in this?" Tre asked. "Oh shit," he said as he fell out laughing. "I forgot that she stole one of your baby daddies from you."

"That bitch didn't steal anything from me. Dalvin is a hoe just like her and they deserve each other. That bitch ain't doing nothing, but using his dumb ass. He's taking care of her and her kids and barely does anything for the one he has over here," Paige said bitterly.

Paige and Dalvin had been together off and on since they were in high school. They had a ten-year-old son that looked exactly like him. Paige was used to going through the motions with Dalvin, but she never thought that another woman would have him sprung like he was. Even when they broke up they still maintained a friendship, but that went out of the window when Moonie came along. She had him trained better than she had her badass kids. He did whatever she said whenever she said it, something that her own kids didn't do. He used to come around, but even the visits stopped once he got with her. Moonie was older than Paige and Dalvin, but she didn't look like it. After having six kids, that bitch was still pulling niggas in their twenties. She dressed better than most of the women in the projects and her children were always on point too. Paige worked forty hours per week with only three kids, but she still couldn't compete. Moonie was pretty, but she still didn't understand what kind of hold she had on her men, especially her son's father. Dalvin never really did much for her son, but she was hoping for that to change.

"You sound like you're in your feelings," Tre taunted.

"I'm not in my feelings at all. I'm trying to have an adult conversation without arguing all the time. I just want you to be honest with me. I'm a big girl, I can handle whatever you say. Are you messing around with Lamia?" Paige asked while looking Tre directly in his eyes.

"Nope," he replied staring right back at her. He would have loved to tell her the truth, but he had to respect Mia's wishes. Telling Paige was like telling the whole world. The only people who knew about them were Brandis, Rainey and his best friend, Duke, and Mia, wanted it to stay that way. A few people assumed, but nobody really knew for sure.

"Okay, I can see that you're going to keep lying no matter what. My next step is asking her what the deal is. I guess I'll just have to make my nieces beat the truth out of her if she lies to me," Paige threatened.

"Man, I'm trying to stay out of that petty bullshit, but your nieces better stay in their fucking lane. Whatever goes on with us don't have shit to do with them or Lamia. You keep sending them at her and you gon' make me send somebody for their asses. Think I'm playing if you want to," Tre fumed.

"So why are you getting mad if you don't mess with her?"

"That's still my people though. Fuck whatever it is that you talking about."

"Your people my ass," Paige yelled. "You're messing with that lil girl. And from the sound of it you seemed to have caught feelings."

"Let me get out of here and go home. I don't even know why I keep dealing with your simple ass," Tre frowned.

"I don't know why either. It ain't like we fucking no more or nothing. Aside from getting your dick sucked and a hot meal, you don't come over here for nothing else. What, Lamia don't give you no head?" Paige yelled to his departing back.

"Don't flatter yourself ma. It's ain't that hard to find some fire head and a home-cooked meal in the hood. And I'm sure it'll come without all the extra bullshit too," Tre replied.

"Fuck you Tank," she cried angrily. "I'm tired of kissing your ass and begging you to do right by me. You won't be satisfied until another nigga comes along and takes your spot."

Paige slammed her door and flopped down on her sofa with a defeated attitude. She loved Trevon to death, but his lack of commitment was starting to get old. She knew that he was young when she first pursued him, but he carried himself like a grown man even back then. At one time, they were inseparable, but those days seemed to be long gone. There was a point in time that he would give her the world without her having to ask for it. He would go to the mall and bring back bags for her even if she wasn't with him. He would spend days inside of her apartment without even thinking about going outside. They used to have date nights at least twice a week and she missed that more than anything. He used to say that he wanted her to have his baby, but that would never happen since they barely had sex anymore. Paige tried to keep an open mind about everything, but she was no fool. There was definitely another woman in the picture and her woman's intuition was telling her that it was Lamia. There was no one else that she could think of. She was fully aware that she was Tank's God sister, but that didn't mean a damn thing to her. They weren't related by blood, so they were free to do as they pleased. It was crazy because she used to really like Lamia at one time. She would always talk to her, Rainey and Brandis whenever she saw them. It wasn't until about a year ago that she started to notice the changes.

Mia was a pretty girl and her shape was one that most women paid money to obtain. Tank no longer treated Mia like the little girl who spent weekends at his house. He started to get overprotective of her. He didn't want any of his friends talking to her, but it wasn't a problem if they tried to get at Rainey. Paige noticed the way he would look at her and it wasn't like it was before. He started doing little things for her like a man did for his woman. Mia started driving his car and he dropped everything the minute she called him. Whenever he showed up with something new, Mia would have the exact same thing. Paige called him out on it, but he always denied it. She'd even reduced herself to playing on Mia's phone whenever he wasn't around, and she always heard his voice in the background. Of course, he always used the fact that she was his God sister as his defense and that made it harder for Paige to find out the truth. After sulking for almost an hour, Paige grabbed her phone to call her nieces. She didn't have any proof about Tank and Mia's relationship yet, but that wasn't going to stop her from finding some.

Chapter 3

"Tre wait, you're going too deep," Mia protested while pushing on his chest. He was on top of her in the spare bedroom and they were working up a sweat. Von and Cheryl had gone out for a while and he was knocking at the spare bedroom door a few minutes later. Brandis was spending the weekend over with her, but she was sleeping in the other guest room. Rainey decided to stay home that weekend, so Brandis used the room that she usually occupied.

"Move your hand Mia, I wasn't complaining when you were on top," Tre replied. He begged Mia to slow down when she was on top of him, but she ignored him and kept going. Then when he started to get too loud, she shoved her underwear in his mouth to quiet him down. She had him feeling like she had the upper hand at first, but she couldn't handle it once the tables turned on her. She thought it was funny when she was in control, but she wasn't laughing any more.

"Ughh, you're hurting me Tre, I'm serious," Mia complained. He had her legs folded up like a pretzel while he hit spots that she didn't even know existed. It was a mixture of pleasure and pain, but the pain was quickly winning the battle. She was sure to be sore the next day if he continued to assault her hidden treasure the way he was doing.

"Damn this feels good," Tre panted as he continued to bang Mia mercilessly. "Don't make me stop please. I promise I'll kiss it for you when I'm done."

Hearing him say that made Mia suck it up and endure the temporary discomfort. Tre's tongue game was something serious and she couldn't pass that up. He didn't know what he was doing in the beginning, but he quickly learned what it took to have her climbing the walls. He was the first and only man to go down on her, so she didn't have anyone else to compare him to anyway. In her eyes, he was all that and more.

"And make sure you pull out," Mia commanded. She heard how short and labored his breathing was, so she knew that it wouldn't be much longer before he came.

"You're still taking your pills right?" he asked looking down at her.

"Yeah Tre, but--" Mia started before he cut her off.

"But nothing, I'm not pulling out," Tre replied. "I'm about to come," he yelled right before his body stiffened up and he spilled his seeds inside of her. He collapsed on top of Mia and pulled her close to him.

"We're going to have to start using condoms. Just because I'm on the pill doesn't mean that I won't get pregnant. I keep telling you to pull out," Lamia fussed.

"A condom won't keep you from getting pregnant either. They break all the time. And, you promised me that we wouldn't have to use condoms if I went and got tested for everything. I got my clean bill of health, so we're good."

"That don't mean shit if you're still out there fucking Paige and the rest of them nasty hoes."

"I'm not having sex with nobody else, but I know how to strap up if I do," Tre said getting up from the bed. He went into the adjoining bathroom to get a warm towel and started to clean Mia up.

"So you're admitting that you sleep with other people?" she asked him. He ignored her question and went to put the towel back in the bathroom.

"Are you ignoring me Tre?" Mia asked.

"I really don't know what you want from me Lamia, but I'm tired of playing this game with you. Until you decide what we have going on here, I'm free to do whatever I want. I've made it clear that I want us to be together, but the ball is in your court. Until you make a decision don't question me about nothing."

"Okay cool, but that goes both ways. Don't flip out when you see me talking to somebody else and stop checking other niggas when they call my phone. You don't ask me any questions and I'll do the same for you," Mia countered.

"Nah, that's bullshit. I know where I want to be and I'm not confused about it. You're the one that wants to keep us a secret. If you can be in the open messing with other niggas you can be in the open with me."

"But it's not that easy for us Tre."

"Why not?" he inquired. "I'm not saying that Von won't be pissed, but he'll get over it eventually. I'm his only son and he loves you like a daughter. He might not understand in the beginning, but he'll have no choice but to come around.

"But what if he doesn't? I just can't take that chance Tre. Sometimes I feel like Von is all I have as far as parents go. Lamar is a dope fiend and Moonie don't even know where I am most of the time. I don't want to push away the only positive adult influence that I have in my life," Mia reasoned with him.

"I understand that Mia, but how long do you think this is going to last? I would rather for us to tell him than to let him find out on his own or from somebody else. He's really going to be pissed then."

"I know, I guess we just have to pick the right time to tell him."

"Okay, I'm just waiting on you. You know I'm not going anywhere," Tre replied seriously.

"You promise?" Mia asked him.

"I promise," he replied while looking her in the eye.

"And what about your other promise?" Mia inquired.

"What other promise?"

Instead of replying, she gapped her legs open and pointed to her love box. "You can kiss it now."

"I got you," he smiled while crawling over to her. He threw her legs over his shoulders and proceeded to make good on his promise, until Mia fell asleep. He had to wake her a few hours later for them to take a shower, but she was out again in no time.

Mia woke up around noon the next day to an empty bed. Her bladder was full and her stomach was growling as if she hadn't eaten in days. After taking a shower and changing her bedclothes, she and Tre went to sleep around three that morning. Most times Tre would dip out early before Von got up, but she was too tired to notice when he left. They heard when him and Cheryl come back home, but they went straight to Von's bedroom like they always did.

"That bastard," Mia mumbled when she got out of bed and almost hit the floor. Her body was sore and her kitty was throbbing from the hurting that Tre had put on it a few hours prior. She knew that she would feel it later, but she didn't think it would be that bad. After doing her morning hygiene, she threw on some sweat pants and headed down the hall. She heard Cheryl's loud mouth coming from the kitchen before she even got in there. When she heard Cheryl's daughter, London's voice, she wanted to turn around and go right back to bed. As much as she couldn't stand Cheryl, it was even worse with London. She had a huge crush on Tre and she didn't mind letting it be known. She constantly flirted with him no matter who was around to witness it. Cheryl had been trying to hook them up for the longest, but Tre wasn't interested, or at least that's what he claimed. Mia couldn't wait until Von got tired of Cheryl and sent her home for a while like he usually did. They weren't in a relationship, but she was trying her best to change that. Von had a few other females that he entertained from time to time, but Tanya was Mia's favorite, maybe because she was also her Godmother. Tanya grew up with Von and Mia's father, and she and Von dated for a while before he got locked up. By the time he came home, Tanya had gotten married, but they still remained close. Tanya's son, Duke and Tre were best friends and she, too, looked out for him while his father was in prison. Once Tanya got divorced, she and Von rekindled their old flame, but they didn't put any labels on what they had. They spent time with each

41

other, but they also dated other people in the process. Cheryl hated Tanya and that only made Mia love her more.

"You must have been tired Mimi," Von commented when Lamia entered the kitchen. "I've never known you to sleep that long."

"Yeah, I was tired," Mia replied, while trying not to laugh at the smirk on Tre and Brandis' faces. She ignored Cheryl and London just as they always did to her. She could feel them staring at her, but she refused to acknowledge their presence.

"You sure you're alright Mimi? Why does it look like you're limping?" Von asked. Tre and Brandis roared with laughter after that and Mia couldn't help but to laugh with them. Tre fell out of his seat and was on the floor holding his stomach from laughing so hard.

"Shut up, y'all make me sick," Mia giggled.

"What did we miss? What's the joke?" London asked with a confused look on her face.

"Don't even ask," Von replied. "It's always some side bar conversations going on with them."

"You good Mia?" Tre asked with a huge grin on his face. Mia flipped him her middle finger and slowly took her seat at the island.

"What did you cook Von?" Mia asked.

"They wanted grits with cheese and hot sausage. You want some?"

"No, I wanted an omelet," Mia pouted.

"What's wrong with what he cooked?" London asked. "It's so good."

"Like I said, I want an omelet," Mia snapped with a roll of her eyes.

"I got you baby girl. I'm about to fix it for you right now," Von chimed in. He knew that Mia didn't care for Cheryl and her daughter, so he tried to keep the peace between the three of them. He hated to say it, but if it ever came down to it, Cheryl and London would get the boot before his baby girl did. Mia had been through enough in her young life and he wasn't about to let her go through anything else if he could help it.

"So, can I look forward to a hot meal from you one of these days Tank?" London asked flirtatiously. "Von knows his way around the kitchen, so I'm sure you have some skills too."

"Nah, I don't really do the cooking thing. I'll eat out before I burn up the house," he chuckled. Mia looked at the smile that covered his face and he quickly wiped it off. He was used to London flirting, but he didn't want to make Lamia mad.

"Don't worry, I know how to cook," she said winking at him. This time he turned his head without replying to what she said. He felt Mia's eyes burning a hole through him, but he refused to make eye contact with her. When the doorbell rang, he jumped up to answer it since he so desperately needed the temporary distraction.

"Hey Duke," Mia smiled when her other God brother walked into the kitchen.

"What's up sis?" he asked while giving her a one armed hug. Tre walked in behind him and frowned when he saw the two of them embracing. Duke spoke to everybody in the room and took a seat at the table right next to Brandis. He was crushing on Brandis hard, and Rainey was crushing on him.

"What's that?" Cheryl asked referring to the cake dish that Tre now held in his hands.

"My mama sent me over here to bring you your cake Von. She said you better eat it slow because she's not making another one any time soon," Duke laughed. Tanya owned and operated a bakery in the central business district of New Orleans. When her business took off and started doing well, she opened up a few pastry carts in two of the local malls. She made good money and her business was always booming. Nobody could bake a red velvet cake like her and that was Von's favorite.

"Yeah right, your mama knows better than to play with me. I'll have another one in a few days," Von replied while sitting Mia's omelet in front of her.

44

"And ask her where her favorite Godchild's German chocolate cake is. I asked for mine before Von and he got his first," Mia complained with a mouth full of food.

"I just got it like that," Von bragged, while taking the cake from Tre's hands.

"Well, we're about to get going," Cheryl said with an obvious attitude. She stood to her feet with London following her lead.

"Good," Mia mumbled under her breath happy to see them go. If nothing else got Cheryl going, the mention of Tanya's name usually did the trick. Von walked them out while everybody else stayed in the kitchen and continued to talk.

***

"Where are you Mia?" Tre yelled into the phone. He was already aggravated with her and it seemed to take her forever to answer the phone. Cheryl and London were at their house once again, so he and Duke walked to the corner so that he could talk in private. London was damn near begging him to fuck her, but he wasn't in the mood to deal with her at the moment.

"I'm still waiting for Rainey to pick me up. She said that she was on her way over an hour ago, but she's not here yet. Brandis and I have been waiting on her for the longest," Mia answered.

"I'm already pissed off and I feel like you're playing games with me. You missed coming over here last weekend, but I'll be damned if you miss two." Mia had opted to sleep by her brother's house the weekend before and Tre was heated. Rainey came over by herself, but she hung out with Cheryl and London the entire time that she was there. That was cool with Tre because she was starting to get on his nerves anyway. Rainey kept asking him to hook her up with Duke, but the man just wasn't interested. He was tired of telling her that, so he just started ignoring her. What really pissed him off was the fact that she kept trying to push London off on him. He and Mia weren't out in the open, but she knew what the deal was.

"You know that I went by Jabari's last weekend," Mia responded.

"Yeah I know, by all those niggas that run all through his house."

"My brother doesn't have anybody running in and out of his house. You know Tiara don't even play that."

"Yeah, okay," Tre annoyingly replied.

"Whatever Tre, I'll be there as soon as Rainey brings her slow ass on. It's not like I have a car to come on my own. I mean, I can find a ride, but you probably won't like who I get it from," Mia snickered.

"You call yourself trying to be funny Lamia?" Tre shouted angrily. "Tell Rainey don't even worry about picking you up. I'm on my way."

"What happened?" Duke questioned once Tre hung up the phone.

"I'm going to pick her stupid ass up from The Court. Brandis is with her, so I know you're coming."

"Hell yeah," Duke smiled while walking back to Tre's silver Dodge Challenger.

It only took about fifteen minutes to get to Lamia's apartment and her and Brandis were already standing outside waiting on them. She and Tre argued all the way back to Von's house, while Duke tried his best to get with Brandis. When they got there, Rainey was just pulling up as well.

"I could have picked you up Mia. You act like it would have killed you to wait a few more minutes," she said when everybody got out of the car. She immediately noticed Duke talking to Brandis and that scene didn't sit too well with her.

"I told her to tell you not to worry about it. You were taking too long," Tre replied with an aggravated look on his face. He was hoping that Cheryl and London would be gone, but he wasn't so lucky. He really hoped that Von took them out somewhere just so that he and Mia could have some alone time. He was tempted to get a room for the weekend, but he needed to run the idea by Lamia first. It was times like these that he wished for a place of his own. At least then, they wouldn't have to worry about being bothered.

"I just asked Von to call you. Are you ready for our double date to the movies?" London asked Tre as soon they walked into Von's house. Mia stopped in her tracks to see just how he was going to respond. Brandis stopped, too, because she wanted to make sure that her friend didn't snap on anybody. Tre felt like all eyes were on him, but the only person's he could feel were Mia's. He didn't know what the hell London was talking about, but he was about to find out. He had to get it straight before Mia flipped out on him.

"What double date?" Tre asked looking around the room. Von was trying hard not to laugh, but he couldn't help it. He and Cheryl had already planned to go to the movies and London invited herself along. She begged him to ask Tre to come, but he refused to get involved. When she started saying that they were going on a double date, Von knew that his son wouldn't like that too much.

"My mama and Von are going to the movies, so I figured that you and I could tag along with them. If Rainey and Duke come then we can make it a triple date," London joked.

"That's cool with me," Rainey said making Mia's pressure rise. Duke was looking to Tre for some help and he quickly got the hint.

"Nah, I think I'll pass, but y'all have fun," Tre said right as Mia was walking away. She dropped her bags in the hallway and went straight outside to the backyard. She was ready to snap and fresh air was all that she could think of.

"Don't say shit to me," Mia snapped through clenched teeth as soon as Tre walked up on her.

"Mia, I swear I don't what the hell she's talking about. I never made plans to go nowhere with her ass. You heard what she just said. She took it upon herself to do that shit. Why would I beg you to come over here if I already had plans to go somewhere with her?" Tre whispered.

"That man didn't make any plans with her crazy ass Mia. I've been here all day and they barely said two words to each other. That bitch is on some fatal attraction stalker type shit," Duke said defending his friend.

"And Rainey is a no good bitch with her thirsty ass," Brandis pointed out.

"Baby, please say something," Tre begged Mia. Her silence was making him nervous because he didn't know what she was thinking.

"Let's go," Mia said after a few more minutes of being quiet.

"Go where?" Tre asked her.

"They wanna go to the movies so let's go to the movies. Fuck I look like letting you go anywhere with that hoe by yourself. Just know that you and that bitch are playing with the right one," Mia informed him.

"I'm not trying to play with you at all. I got put up in some bullshit that I didn't know anything about," Tre replied.

"Are you sure about this Mia? I'm broke as hell right now, so maybe we should just stay here," Brandis replied feeling slightly embarrassed. Mia had already given her something to wear for the weekend and she didn't feel right asking her for anything else.

"I got y'all, let's just go before I get blamed for something else," Tre replied right as Rainey walked over to them.

"Y'all are making yourselves look real suspect right now. You claim you don't want anybody to know what's going on, but you almost went off on London for wanting Tank to go to the movies with her," Rainey said to Mia.

"You really got me fucked up too Rainey. What makes you think that I would be okay with Tre going anywhere with London? You know off top that I'm not the one for you to play with," Mia barked. Tre looked at her going off and shook his head. Mia was truly Moonie's child and she didn't have a problem saying what was on her mind. Moonie was known for putting bitches in their place and Mia was no different.

"What did I do? I only agreed so that it wouldn't look suspicious. Everybody was just standing there looking at each other crazy. Y'all got Von wondering what the hell is going on. You should know that I would never try to play you like that Lamia," Rainey vowed.

"Baby let's just go," Tre pleaded. "We'll finish talking about this later." If Mia knew that Rainey was in his ear about getting with London, she would drag her all over that yard and he couldn't have that. Mia's hands were nice and he knew that neither Rainey nor London could come close to winning in a fight with her.

They all walked back into the house with somber expressions on their faces, but nobody said anything.

"Y'all good?" Von asked with his eyes trained on his son.

"Yeah, but we all decided to go with y'all to the movies. We don't have anything else to do, so why not," Tre shrugged.

"Well, I guess our double date is out of the question now. Is it cool if I ride with you Tank?" London asked.

"Uh, I got a car full already, so you might have to ride with Von," he replied while unconsciously looking at Lamia. Mia slightly nodded her head letting him know that she was satisfied with his answer.

"Oh, okay, but save me a seat if you get there before us," London requested. He didn't respond to her last comment as he, Mia, Brandis and Duke walked outside to his car.

"I wish the hell you would," Mia said to Tre when they got into the car. He knew better than to reply, so he remained silent and pulled off.

About twenty minutes later, a group of them was purchasing their tickets for the movie. Mia and Brandis wanted candy, so Tre and Duke stood in line to get some snacks for them. London and Rainey walked in right when they were paying for their items, followed by Von and Cheryl.

"I didn't want anything Tank, but thanks for offering," Rainey spat sarcastically.

"Girl, stop overdoing it all the time. If you wanted something all you had to do was ask, just like Mia and Brandis did."

"Closed mouths don't get fed," Von butted in. "What do y'all want?" he asked Rainey, London and Cheryl. Once everybody got their snacks, they all walked into the theater and tried to find some seats. It wasn't crowded, so they didn't have to look hard. Mia didn't say anything, but she was waiting to see if London would try to sit next to Tre. She was also waiting to see if he would let it happen. He was no fool though. He went to an empty row and made sure that he sat in the last seat by the aisle. He pulled Mia to the seat next to him, followed by Brandis and Duke. Since both of the girls hand handbags, Brandis moved over one and let her and Mia's items sit in the empty chair. London and Rainey sat next to Duke, but Cheryl and Von went a few rows down closer to the screen. It was a little after nine that night, but the theater was fairly empty for a weekend. They had a few people scattered throughout the room, but they were in a section all by themselves.

"Are you still mad at me?" Tre asked Mia for the second time since they got there. "I promise you that I didn't do nothing wrong." As soon as the lights went off, he grabbed her hand and held it in his.

"I told you that I'm not mad. I can see that I'll probably have to deal with London sooner or later, but she gets a pass today," Mia replied.

"Let that shit go Lamia. I'm not even trying to go there with her."

"Yeah, so you say. The truth always has a way of being revealed. All I have to do is sit back and wait for it."

"You know I love you right?" Tre asked her. He could barely see her because of the darkness, but he turned his head in her direction anyway.

"Yeah I know and I love you too," Mia replied.

"Okay, well show me," Tre said with a sneaky grin.

"Please don't start up with that again," Mia begged.

"No, I'm not talking about us telling Von."

"What are you talking about then?" She asked.

Instead of answering, he reached over to the empty seat and grabbed his jacket. When he had it over his lap, he unbuckled his pants and pulled his erection out. He grabbed Mia's hand and guided it to where he wanted it to be. He laughed as he watched her eyes light up in the darkness like it was her first time feeling it. She looked around to see if they were being watched, but everybody seemed to be in a world of their own.

"Handle that," Tre smiled while letting his head fall back against the cushioned leather seat. He didn't have to tell Mia twice. She knew just what he liked and she aimed to please, even in the movie theater.

Chapter 4

"Mama, I'm not crazy and I'm telling you what I saw. You had to really pay attention to see it, but she was giving him a hand job right there in the movie theater," London swore to her mother while they sat outside on their patio. Cheryl was at her own house today, but she was pissed because Von was in another one of his moods. He was claiming that he wanted some time alone, but she knew that was code words for he wanted to chill with one of his other bitches. She tried for years to get Von to see that she was worthy of his commitment, but he still wanted to play the field. The other women really didn't bother her that much, but Tanya was the exception. She was the only one that intimidated Cheryl even though she would never admit it. Tanya had known Von longer than she had and they shared a bond because of that. They were both Godparents to Lamia and their sons were best friends. All of those reasons alone kept Tanya around more than she would have liked her to be. Cheryl hated how Von looked at her, but there was nothing that she could do about it. At the end of the day, Von was a single man who hadn't agreed to be in a relationship with her or anybody else. No matter how much time they spent together he made it known that he was still up for grabs.

"I don't know London. Tre and Mia are like family and I can't see them doing that, especially in a movie theater," Cheryl replied.

"I keep hearing you say that, but that doesn't change what I know I saw. I think they like each other. I can't believe that you and Von never noticed it before. I really saw it the other day when we went to the movies. Every time I talk to him, he has to look at her before he answers me. And why doesn't he have a girlfriend? As good as he looks, he should have a few bitches hanging around. Something is just not right with that situation," London babbled.

"He doesn't have a girlfriend, but from the way Von talks he does have a lot of female friends. He's not serious with anybody though. That's why I've been telling you to get with his ass. That nigga looks just as good as his daddy and uncles. That lil boy is too fine for words," Cheryl yelled while fanning her face. Von had three brothers, but he was the best looking of them all in Cheryl's opinion.

"Hell yeah he's fine with all those tattoos covering his chest and arms. Everybody says that he looks just like Nelly, but he doesn't think so. It's not like I haven't been trying to get with his ass. I would love to be the one that he comes home to every night, but I feel like he's holding back for some reason. I know you don't think so, but I really think Lamia is the reason," London replied while filing her nails.

"That lil bitch makes me sick," Cheryl frowned. "Von got her thinking that she runs shit over there, but she better not ever play with me. I don't know why he feels like he has to play captain save-a-hoe when it comes to her ass. It's not his fault that her mama is a hoe and her daddy is a crackhead."

"I guess he feels like that because he's her Godfather. I like Rainey, but I don't like Mia's ass either. She's too flip by the mouth."

"I like Rainey too, but I hate how Von treats Lamia better than her. He's always saying how Mia has it so hard, but I can't tell. She wears better clothes than me and I work every day," Cheryl replied.

She hated how Von catered to Lamia's every need, but she knew not to say that in front of him. He was always saying that Rainey had her mother and stepfather, but Mia didn't have anyone. Cheryl really couldn't stand her because she was always throwing Tanya up in her face. She knew that she was doing it on purpose, but Von didn't see anything wrong with it. Then Tank being best friends with Tanya's son didn't help the situation much either.

"I guess we won't be going over there for a while, huh?" London asked.

"Girl, you know how Von is when he wants some different pussy. He probably has Tanya's ugly ass over there or he's probably at her house. That's why Tank can't commit to one woman. He's following right in his father's footsteps."

"I don't understand why Von just won't make things official with y'all. You're always over there and y'all spend a lot of time together. I don't see what the big deal is," London wondered.

"Just like you're trying to make Tank yours, I'm trying to do the same with his daddy. I'm confident that he'll come around soon. I just have to be patient," Cheryl reasoned. She'd helped Von out significantly with growing his and Tre's businesses and she felt like he owed her for that and so much more. She would never say that to his face, but she was hoping that he would see it for himself, sooner rather than later. He was always saying how much he appreciated her, but she wanted him to show her and stop telling her.

"I'm wearing Tank down, I can just feel it. One of us has to get our foot in the door. That way we can help to pull the other one in," London smiled.

"That sounds like a plan to me girlfriend," Cheryl agreed while giving her daughter a high five.

After being Von's insignificant other for the past five years, Cheryl was nowhere near ready to give up on him. Unlike London's father, Von was everything that she could ever want in a man. Not only was he very pleasing to the eyes, but he had more money than any man that she's ever been with. It wasn't that Cheryl needed it because she had her own. She'd been a small business consultant who worked from home for almost twenty years. She was her own boss and she set her own schedule. Still, it was always nice to go out with a man and not have to worry about spending your own money. Von knew how to wine and dine her as if she was the only woman in the world. He had no problem rolling out the red carpet for the women in his life, but she was tired of sharing the spotlight with all of the others. She tried her best not to nag him about it, but she made sure to let him know how she felt whenever the subject came up. Cheryl wasn't used to losing and she didn't plan on losing Von to Tanya or anybody else.

***

"Moonie c'mon, I have less than an hour to make it to my appointment on time," Mia yelled to her mother. She had an appointment with her gynecologists and she needed a refill on her birth control pills. She'd been trying to wake Moonie up for thirty minutes straight, but she had yet to get up. She'd gone to the club the night before, so she was probably just now going to sleep.

"Damn Mia, can't you reschedule until tomorrow or something?" Moonie groaned. "I'm tired."

"This is my rescheduled appointment. Did you forget that you cancelled last week too? I took my last pill this morning and he won't give me a refill without a checkup."

"Well take my truck and go by yourself. I just got in the bed and I'm not getting up any time soon," Moonie replied as she threw the covers over her head.

"I can't go by myself Moonie. I have to have an adult with me in order to be seen," Mia said on the verge of tears. She had to go through this every time her mother had to take her somewhere. She used to beg Moonie not to go out the night before her appointments for this very same reason. Most times, she gave herself a two-hour head start just to make sure she got her up on time.

"Well I don't know what to tell you. Call Von and see if he can take you. You need to reschedule like I told you. Dr. Irvin won't mind. I used to do the shit all the time," Moonie muttered.

"Don't even worry about it. Where are your keys? I'll find somebody to go with me," Mia sniffled as she wiped a few tears from her eyes. She didn't even wait for Moonie to answer before she spotted the keys on the dresser and snatched them up. She walked out of her mother's room and slammed the door as hard as she could. Aside from her brother's girlfriend, Tiara, Mia really didn't have anyone else to call on. It was a little after nine, so she knew that Tiara was probably still sleeping. Besides, her brothers and sisters were at Tiara and

Jabari's house and she didn't want to take her away from them just to go with her to the clinic. She could have called Tre or Von, but she didn't feel comfortable with a man going to the clinic with her. All of her friends were the same age as her and she was too embarrassed to ask one of their mothers to do what Moonie should have been doing. She thought about Tanya, but again she was too embarrassed to make the call. It was last minute anyway, so her Godmother probably already had something else to do. When Mia's phone rang, she was almost tempted not to answer it until she saw who it was calling. She was desperate right now and he would just have to do for now.

"Hey daddy," Mia said when she answered the phone for Lamar.

"What's up baby?" Lamar asked his only daughter.

"Nothing, but daddy I need a big favor from you if you can do it."

"Okay, what's up?"

"I have a doctor's appointment and Moonie don't want to wake up to take me. Can you sign me in so I can see the doctor? You don't have to come in the room or nothing. You can just wait out front until I'm done. I have Moonie's truck and I can pick you up. It won't take long I promise," Mia rambled.

"Alright baby girl. I'm at home and I'm dressed. Just swing through and come get me," Lamar replied.

"Okay daddy, I'm on my way right now. Thank you so much, I really appreciate this," Mia said right before she hung up the phone. She still had about thirty minutes to get there and she was confident that she would make it there on time. After locking the front door, she ran to Moonie's new pearl white Escalade and headed to her father's house. She looked like a toddler behind the wheel of the huge truck, but she knew how to handle it as if it was made just for her. One of Moonie's boyfriends taught her how to drive when she was fourteen years old and she was a pro at it now. Von took her to get her license on her seventeenth birthday and she'd been on the go ever since.

About three hours later, Mia and her father were pulling back up to her apartments. She made it to her appointment on time and filled her prescription for more birth control pills. She hated that Lamar had to come into the room while she talked to her doctor, but a parent or guardian had to be present at the time. Afterwards, Lamar took her out to lunch at Chili's and they had a good time just talking to one another. Most times Mia saw her father at least three times a week since he didn't live that far from where she lived. He would always walk over to The Court to visit her or chill with some of his friends that lived in the area. Von made sure they stayed in contact even if he had to pick Lamar up and bring him to his house. When Lamar wasn't high, he usually spent more time with Mia than Moonie ever did. He would always take her out to eat or sometimes they would catch a movie together. Moonie thought that since she bought her everything she wanted, she was doing her job. Mia never remembered spending time with her mother and her siblings were no different. She would pay for them to go with someone else, but she never took them anywhere herself.

"Where is your lazy ass mama at?" Lamar said when he walked into the apartment behind Mia.

"She's probably still in the bed knowing her," Mia assumed. "You want something to drink daddy?"

"Yeah, what y'all got in there?" Lamar asked.

"Dalvin probably left some of his beer in there. Let me go see," Mia said walking away.

She was happy to be spending time with her father and she was even happier because he was sober. A few times when he came to see her, he would be itching like crazy or nodding off as they talked. Sometimes he would show up with fresh track marks, but that wasn't the case today. Von often scolded him for coming around her when he was high, but that never stopped him from doing it.

"Here you go," Mia said while handing Lamar an ice-cold bottle of Heineken.

"Thank you baby, I appreciate it," Lamar replied. "Go call your mama for me."

"No daddy, I don't even want to talk to her right now."

"Well I do and she better bring her ass out here. Mya!" Lamar yelled calling Moonie by her real name. Besides Mia's grandmother, he was the only one who did. They waited for a few minutes, but Moonie never came out of the room.

"She's probably still sleeping," Mia remarked.

"Mya!" Lamar yelled again louder than the first time. "She better get her lazy ass up."

Mia didn't say anything, but a few minutes later Moonie came stomping into the living room with a frown covering her pretty face. She still had on her club clothes and her eyes were red and puffy probably from lack of sleep.

"What the fuck are you screaming my name like that for Lamar?" Moonie yelled angrily.

"Who the fuck are you talking to like that Mya?" Lamar countered just as upset. Mia was used to them arguing whenever they were in each other's presence, so none of that was new to her. Moonie seemed to hate Lamar for whatever reason and he wasn't too fond of her either. Mia watched as her parents stared each other down for a minute, before Moonie spoke again.

"What do you want Lamar?" Moonie asked again.

"I'm trying to see why you couldn't get up off your lazy ass and take my baby to her doctor's appointment. I didn't mind going, but I'm sure she would have preferred her mama being there with her. Is it that serious for you to go to the club? You go out damn near every night so staying home one time wouldn't have killed you," Lamar snapped.

"Don't come in here trying to tell me how to run my household. I'm the one that takes her to all of her appointments while your ass is probably at home somewhere getting high as a kite. You think because you come around two or three times a week with a few dollars that you're father of the year or something. That lil money ain't shit compared to what I do for Mia."

"You think that buying her clothes and shoes substitutes for you being a good mother? Your seventeen-year-old daughter basically runs this household because you're always shaking your ass in the club or smiling in a different nigga's face."

"And you sticking a needle in your arm damn sure don't make you a good father. Von is more of a father to her than you've ever been. Looks like I fucked the wrong friend," Moonie growled. Mia jumped up and grabbed her father's arm when he attempted to get to her mother.

"Daddy no!" she yelled while pulling him towards the door.

"Don't hold his bitch ass back Mia. I want him to put his hands on me in my house. The coroners will be carrying his crackhead ass out of here in a body bag," Moonie swore.

"Fuck that gold digging bitch!" Lamar yelled angrily. "As long as I had money that bitch couldn't get enough of me."

"Yeah, but all of your money goes to the dope man now," Moonie laughed loudly.

"Come on and let me walk you outside daddy," Mia said while leading her daddy out of the front door.

"I'm sorry that you had to see that Mia, but I hate that bitch. As much as I used to love Mya, I swear I never thought that it would come to this. I know I'm not the best father in the world, but she's a sad ass mama. I mean, what kind of mother wants her kids to call her by her nickname? She's too busy trying to be y'all friend and that's what the problem is," Lamar fussed.

Mia felt like crying, but she held her composure as best she could. Both of her parents made some valid points about each other, but it shouldn't have been done right in front of her. They never took the time out to see how what they did affected her and that's what hurt the most. She was tired of being strong for them when they should

66

have been her strength. Most seventeen year olds only had to worry about graduating high school and going to college. If it weren't for Von, Mia would have surely lost her mind a long time ago.

"It's alright daddy, just calm down. Go take a walk and call me later. Maybe we can hook up by Von's house this weekend," Mia suggested.

"Alright baby, I'll talk to you later. Call me if you need anything," Lamar replied as he exited the apartment building. Mia watched him until he was no longer in her line of vision. Although he'd been through a lot in his life, Lamar was still a very handsome man. He still dressed nice, thanks to Von, and he was always clean and smelling good. His hair was always freshly cut because the barbers at Von's shop saw to it. If there was really such a thing as a functioning addict that was what Mia considered her father to be. If you didn't know for a fact that he was on drugs it was really hard to tell. He still had plenty of women and he pulled even more every day.

"I don't know why you called him to take you to your appointment," Moonie said as soon as Mia reentered the apartment.

"I didn't call him, he called me. And why does it matter to you anyway? It's not like you were willing to get up and take me."

"You should have asked Von to take you like I told you to. Now I'll have to hear this shit from him for the next few months," she complained as she stood up from the sofa.

"Von is not my father!" Mia yelled angrily. "Y'all want him to do everything for me as if he already doesn't do enough. I'm your daughter and you should have been there with me, not Von and not Lamar."

"Why not Lamar?" Moonie asked. "You're just as much as his daughter as you is mine. What's wrong with him stepping up to the plate every now and then?"

"You still don't get it. I didn't want my daddy or Von taking me to my gynecologists to get birth control pills. Do you know how embarrassing that shit is? I had to answer questions about my female parts in front of my daddy when my mama should have been there with me instead."

"Why do you always give him a pass? No matter what I do, it's never good enough, but he does the bare minimum and you're happy with that. I'm trying Mia. At least give me credit for that much," Moonie cried.

"I'm not giving either one of y'all a pass because y'all didn't earn it. I didn't ask for any of this and I don't deserve it. I could have been like Jabari, packed up my shit and left a long time ago. I chose to stay here with you because I know you need me to help with the other kids. If I didn't get them up and ready for school most days, they probably wouldn't even go because you don't wake up until noon or later. We keep a house full of food, but can you tell me the last time you cooked a hot meal? If I left it up to you, they would be eating cereal and noodles every day. You begged Dalvin for a two thousand dollar washer and dryer, but you don't even know how to use it. That's because you never do the laundry. That's something else that's all on me. I'm seventeen years old with more responsibilities than women twice my age and that's not fair," Mia replied.

She was unmoved by Moonie's tears because she was used to seeing them by now. Every time they had a conversation about what she was doing wrong as a mother, the waterworks started. She would do right for maybe a week at most and then it was back to the same routine once again.

"I'm sorry Mia," Moonie said while wiping away her tears. "I know that I have to do better and I promise you that I'm going to try. You know I can't function without you being here and I'm happy that you didn't leave. Just give me some time to get it right. Please don't give up on me Mia."

"I haven't given up on you all this time and I never will," Mia said while pulling her mother in for a hug. As much as she hated the things Moonie did, she still loved her no matter what. That was something that she just couldn't help.

Chapter 5

"Nah Mia, you got too much ass for that," Jabari said about the swimsuit that his sister was holding up for him to see. He and his best friend, LJ were having a pool party at a recreation center the next night and he and Mia were in the mall looking for something to wear. Everybody from The Court and everywhere else were going to be in attendance, so he had to make sure that they were on point. He'd already found the perfect tennis shoes to wear, but finding swim attire seemed to be the hardest; not for him because he already had his trunks, but it was a task trying to get Mia right.

"I might as well not even worry about getting a bathing suit. You say the same thing every time I show you something that I like," Mia complained.

"No I don't Mia, but you have to be careful with what you wear. You got a big ass just like Moonie. I don't want to be at my party fighting because some nigga can't keep his hands to himself," Jabari replied.

"Let's just go look somewhere else. We've seen just about everything in here already," Mia said while walking out of the store. Jabari followed behind her until they ended up in Macy's. Mia thumbed through a few things until she came across something that caught her eye. It was a Jessica

Simpson set with mint green boy shorts and the matching fringed halter-top. It was cute and sexy without showing off too much of her backside. She held it up for Jabari to see and she knew from the look on his face that it was the one.

"Yeah Mia, I can see you in that. The shorts are kind of short, but it's better than those little ass bottoms that we saw on some of the other ones," Jabari said nodding his head in approval.

"And they match my mint green and silver Gucci flip flops that Moonie got for me," Mia smiled. "What about Tiara? You need me to help you pick something out for her?"

"Nah, you know how she is. She probably won't even wear a bathing suit. She's too self-conscious about her weight. She don't know the difference between being fat and being thick," Jabari answered.

"She is not fat. That girl is crazy. Tiara has a nice shape," Mia replied.

"I keep telling her that, but she thinks being fine is a size four or six. She makes that size fourteen look good as hell and I don't have any complaints."

Tiara was twenty-two years old with no kids and a good paying job at the post office. She was also a part-time college student studying to be an occupational therapist. Jabari met her about two years ago at a party that Moonie dragged him to.

She seemed to be the only chick there that wasn't having a good time, and Jabari soon found out why. Tiara wasn't like most of the girls her age. She wasn't into the party scene and the night life. That was one of the reasons that he fell in love with her. He approached her right before she left that night and they'd been inseparable ever since. When he got into it with Moonie and moved out a little over a year ago, it was Tiara that begged her parents to let him stay with them until they were able to afford a place of their own. She came from a middle class two-parent home, but she never looked down on him and that meant a lot. Even her family welcomed him and his siblings with opened arms. Being with Tiara had changed Jabari and made him want to do right. She encouraged him to go back to school and get his GED. He still hustled from time to time, but he also held down a decent job working at a chemical plant, thanks to a good word from her father. Tiara also made sure he stayed close with his siblings because she had them over to the house at least twice a week. She was still trying to get him and Moonie to get it right, but that was a situation that would take a lot of work.

"I hope they don't come to the party with all that drama and fighting," Mia said pulling Jabari away from his thoughts.

"LJ and I paid to have detailed security there for the entire party. Von told us that it was better to be safe than sorry, and I agree. We have six police officers for the inside and outside of the building.

72

Since the pool is indoors, I'm thinking that most of the guests will be inside though," Jabari replied.

"Did you invite Marco?" Mia asked him even though she already knew the answer to the question. She looked at him just in time to see his light brown complexion turn red at the mention of his ex-best friend.

"Hell no I didn't invite his ass," he yelled angrily. "And Moonie better not bring her hot ass around there either. I swear I'm telling security to escort her out if she shows up."

"Don't do that Jabari. She's going to be so embarrassed if you play her like that," Mia replied.

"I don't give a damn Mia, that's her whole problem now. She wants to party with us like we're her friends and shit. She's our mother and she needs to start acting like it. After that shit that she and Marco pulled, she had better be lucky that I'm even talking to her ass at all. And after that ass whipping I put on him he better stay his ass away from me too," Jabari fumed.

Marco and Jabari had been best friends since they were in middle school. At twenty-two years old, Marco was only two years older than Jabari and he and his family lived right underneath them for years in the projects. They were always together and they often hung out at each other's houses, until Marco and his family moved uptown three years ago. He and Jabari remained tight and Marco moving away didn't change anything. Marco's mother, Pam always treated Jabari like her son, and Moonie did the same with Marco. Well at least she did up until a year and a half ago. Jabari didn't know when, but somewhere along the line, Moonie stopped looking at Marco as a son and decided that she wanted him to be her man instead. It went over Jabari's head for a long time until he came home early one day and saw his best friend coming out of Moonie's room butt ass naked. After the initial shock wore off, he beat Marco's ass all over Moonie's living room and out into the front of the building, just as naked as he was when he caught him. He had it out with Moonie, packed up his clothes and moved out the very same night. He'd been there to visit a few times, but he never went back to live with her after that. Marco tried to get Jabari to forgive him, but it never happened. He apologized to him a million times, but he didn't want to hear it. Even though Marco and Moonie stopped dealing with each other, the damage was already done. To Jabari, that was the most embarrassing thing that could ever happen to him and it was unforgivable. Mia made him sit down and talk to Moonie, but their relationship was never the same after that. Moonie did what she usually did when she was wrong and broke down crying, but that still didn't move Jabari one bit. Marco was still around, but Jabari ignored him as if he never knew him at all.

"I know that you were hurt about everything that happened, but you have to learn to forgive Jabari. I know that you'll never forget it, but don't let what happened keep having control over your emotions like this."

"That situation did more than just hurt me Mia. That shit messed with me mentally. I considered Marco my brother at one time. Imagine how I felt seeing him coming out of Moonie's room with no clothes on. That was somebody that she referred to as her son at one time, but then she turned around and slept with him anyway. So again, if either of them shows up at my party I'm having their asses thrown the fuck out," Jabari promised.

"I'll make sure I tell her not to come. She won't have anybody to keep the kids anyway since all of us are going to be at the party," Mia said after a while.

"That's the least she can do. You have her damn kids more than her. I don't know why you let her do that shit to you Mia. You be sitting inside babysitting while she runs the streets with her men. Moonie is too damn selfish if you ask me."

"She doesn't make me babysit Jabari, but I help her out sometimes if she asks me to. If I have somewhere to go and they're not with you and Tiara, she won't go out at all. She doesn't just leave them with anybody and I do give her credit for that much," Mia said.

"Yeah and that's about all I give her ass credit for too," Jabari snapped as he and Mia headed for the exit. "She fucks up everything. She ran Des and Mitch away and she's the reason why Lamar is hooked on drugs. If my daddy wasn't in jail for life, she probably would have done him in too."

"Lamar being on drugs is not her fault. You know he had a hard time coping with Reynard's death. And Des was just as bad as Moonie was," Mia said taking her mother's side. Desmond was one of Moonie's ex-boyfriends. He was also the father of Moonie's two middle kids. He took good care of Moonie and her kids, but he had a problem keeping his hands to himself. Moonie was a street runner when she met him, but he tried his best to slow her down. When he saw that changing Moonie was almost impossible, he packed up his clothes and kept it moving. He still took very good care of his kids and Moonie was satisfied with that.

"Stop always taking her side Mia. You always do that and you know she's not right."

"I didn't say that she's always right Jabari, but damn. Do you really hate her that much?" Mia asked while looking over at him.

"Honestly, I don't hate her at all. I tried to, but it's impossible for me to do. Moonie's really not a bad person, she just makes bad decisions. I understand that she had a baby when she was just a baby herself, but that's not an excuse."

"It's like she missed out on her childhood and now she's trying to get it back. She makes me sick sometimes, but I can't help but love her ass," Mia remarked.

"I love her too, but she needs to get it together. I really wish she would have stayed with Mitch. She did that dude wrong, but he hung in there until he couldn't take it anymore. He wasn't just good to his kids, he was good to all of us," Jabari replied.

Anthony Mitchell, or Mitch, was one of Moonie's ex-boyfriends. He was the father of her two youngest kids, Anthony Jr., and Anika. He and Moonie dated off and on for years until her trifling ways finally ran him off. At thirty-eight years old, Mitch was settled and he wanted a woman that was the same. Moonie went out four to five times a week, so he knew that she wasn't the one. That didn't stop him from falling in love and wanting to settle down with her though. He was hoping to be the one to change her, but that was damn near impossible to do. Even though he had a girlfriend, he was still hoping that one day he and Moonie would get back together. He still took care of her and his kids and even helped out with all the others. He always told her that when she got tired of playing around in the streets that he would be there waiting for her.

"I wish she would have stayed with him too. He's still trying to be with her, so maybe it'll happen one day. Anybody is better than Dalvin's stupid ass. Moonie got him so gone until it's ridiculous," Mia said.

"That nigga is just dumb. He's struggling to pay his own bills because he's trying to take care of

Moonie, and she's still messing over him with other dudes," Jabari said shaking his head.

"That's all on them, but thanks for getting me and Brandis a bathing suit. I know she's going to be happy when I take it to her," Mia said moving on to another subject.

"You know that's not a problem. Brandis is my girl with her lil thin ass," Jabari laughed. "And you know my boy, Cam has been asking me if you were coming through."

"I don't know why he's asking about me. Camden has a live-in girlfriend and a baby. I'm not trying to have no baby mama drama in my life."

"I hear you, but I'm only saying that he was asking about you. I really don't want you to mess with none of my friends anyway. I'll have to put the beat down on one of them niggas if they play with you," Jabari swore right as they got in his car to leave.

"That makes two of us. All of your friends are dogs anyway. Camden got a woman in his bed every night, but he's trying to creep with me. But he'll swear up and down that he loves her to death."

"Just because he cheats doesn't mean that he don't love his girl. I know I love Tiara like I've never loved another woman, but that don't stop me from dipping out every now and again."

"So you cheat on Tiara?" Mia questioned with raised brows. Jabari had never given her any indications that he would do something like that to his girlfriend. She'd never even seen them argue, and they were always happy when she was around. Maybe they were putting on a front, but they did a good job of hiding their problems if they had any.

"It's not like I set out to cheat on her nothing like that. Sometimes shit happens, but that don't mean that I love her any less. Now don't get it twisted, I would never leave my girl behind none of these hoes out here, but temptation is a muthafucka though," he replied honestly.

"So you're not happy with Tiara?" Mia asked just to be sure.

"Yeah I'm happy with her. Being unhappy is not the only reason why people cheat Mia. A few times the opportunity presented itself and I went for it. It wasn't about love or feelings, it was just sex. It's been a few months since I did some shit like that though. I really don't plan on even going there again. Tiara would kill me if she found out."

"And you know that her feelings would be hurt. I get what you're saying Jabari, but none of them hoes, as you call them, are worth losing Tiara. Y'all have a good thing going and you're willing to throw it away for a few quick nuts."

"I'm not throwing anything away. It's not like any of the females that I was with were single. They all have boyfriends or husbands. We got what we wanted from each other and we moved on," Jabari shrugged.

"Exactly how many females were there?" Mia wanted to know.

"Damn you're nosey, but it was only two," he answered. "And let's talk about you Mia? You want to be all in my business, but I see you keep texting somebody every few minutes. Who is this nigga that got all of your attention?"

"Now you're worrying about the wrong thing," Mia laughed right as they pulled up to The Court.

"Oh, so now that we're talking about you the conversation is over."

"You got that right. Let me know if you need me and Brandis to come early and help you with anything tomorrow," Mia said as she got out of the car and headed straight to Brandis' apartment. Jabari was about to pull off and leave, but he changed his mind at the last minute. He decided to go and see Moonie and his sisters and brothers instead. He thought long and hard about what Mia had said, but he was still torn. He knew that he had to get it right with Moonie eventually, but he couldn't make any promises on how long that would take. Just like with a recovering addict, he had to take the situation one day at a time.

Chapter 6

The next day, Mia, Rainey, Brandis and unfortunately London, arrived at Jabari's party about thirty minutes after it started. When Rainey showed up to get them with London in her front seat, Mia was ready to go off. It wasn't until they started talking that she realized that Von was the one who'd invited her to the event. He was helping out on the grills, so Cheryl would probably be there too. Tanya was out of town, but if she wasn't, Mia would have made sure to invite her as well.

"Let me go find my future baby daddy," London laughed when they got out of the car. Rainey looked over at Mia because she knew that she didn't like what was being said. London looked pretty decent in her one-piece bathing suit with the sides cut out, but she didn't have shit on Mia. Even Brandis' slender frame was looking right in her hot pink two-piece set. Rainey overdid it as usual. She was a little self-conscience about the few stretch marks on her belly, so she wore a polka dot one piece with a sarong tied snugly around her waist. Mia laughed at the huge floppy hat and oversized glasses that adorned her small round face. All of the other girls had on flip-flops, but Rainey chose to wear her tall rhinestone gladiator sandals instead. Then to top it off, she had a huge polka dot straw purse to go along with it all. When they walked into the building, all eyes were on them, but Mia was busy looking around for her brother. Jabari and LJ went all out with all the colorful strobe lights they had lighting up the otherwise dark room. She spotted Von talking to a group of men with Cheryl holding tightly onto his arm. She led the pack as they headed straight to where her Godfather was standing.

"Hey everybody," Mia spoke as soon as she approached the group. Everybody spoke, but Cheryl just looked her up and down like she was seeing her for the first time. When Von looked at her she knew that he was about to go in about what she was wearing.

"Now you know I'm not feeling that lil ass bathing suit that you have on," Von said as he frowned up at Lamia. "You should have put on a t-shirt or something Mimi."

"Von, nobody wears t-shirts over their bathing suits anymore," Mia laughed.

"I don't care about what everybody else is doing, I'm talking about you. You know I don't like all that skimpy shit that y'all young girls are out here wearing. Look at Rainey, she looks good and nothing is showing on her. Your ass is built just like Moonie, so you should know better," Von continued to fuss.

"Okay and on that note, I'm going to look for Jabari," Mia said as she walked away grabbing Brandis' hand.

"Yeah, your ass better run," Von yelled after her. She ignored him and continued in the opposite direction. She was happy when London and Rainey didn't follow. She wasn't in the mood for her unwanted shadows at the moment. Besides, she was two seconds from popping London right in her mouth if she kept making slick remarks about Tre. Mia spotted her brother on the other side of the room, but she had to pass by Tre and his friends in order to get to him.

"Got damn Mia, that ass is sitting right in that bathing suit," Tre's friend, Roland yelled as soon as she got close to them. When Mia told Tre about some of his friends trying to get with her, Ro was at the top of that list. He was always making slick comments about her shape or he would say something about the two of them hooking up. He looked like a light-skinned frog, so that would never happen on her watch.

"You better chill out Ro," Tre said angrily. "I told you about playing with her like that."

"Man I'm sorry, but lil sis can get it," he replied while grabbing his crotch.

"Nigga," Tre yelled while walking over to him.

"I'm just playing man, calm down," Ro said with a chuckle as he ran in the opposite direction. Their other friends followed behind him, leaving Mia and Brandis alone with Duke and Tre.

"Why the fuck do you have this lil shit on Mia?" Tre snapped the minute they were alone. He saw her when she first walked in and he wanted to drag her ass right back out and make her go home. He was bound to be fighting all night if niggas kept checking her out the way were. Jabari had the police all over the place, but he didn't care. Jail was nothing new to him anyway.

"This is not little. At least I have on shorts and not a bikini bottom like most of the chicks here. You always have something to say, but it would've been cool if you saw another bitch with this on. You would have been breaking your neck trying to sneak a peek," Mia replied.

"What's up sis?" Duke asked trying to defuse the situation. He walked over to Mia and pulled her into a hug.

"I'm sorry Duke, what's up?" Mia replied hugging him back.

"Alright nigga that's enough, damn," Tre snapped not feeling the exchange between the two of them.

"C'mon bruh, now you know it ain't even like that. That's my God sister," Duke replied.

"And?" Tre questioned. "You of all people should know that don't mean shit to me. She's my God sister too."

"Seriously Tre? That wasn't even called for," Mia said angrily as she walked away followed by Brandis.

"Stupid ass," Tre fumed as soon as she left.

"Man you know you were wrong for that shit that you just said," Duke commented. "Mia is like family and I would never play no games like that with her."

"No offense bruh, but that's the same shit I used to say," Tre said while keeping his eyes trained on Mia as she walked over to her brother.

"What it do Mia?" Jabari said when his sister and her best friend walked over to him and his boys.

"Nothing, but y'all got it jumping in here. Where is Tiara?" Mia asked.

"She's around here somewhere with her friends," Jabari replied.

"So you don't see me standing right here Mia?" Cam said interrupting their conversation. "You can't speak?"

"You saw me standing here too, but you didn't open your mouth either," Mia sassily replied.

"What's up pretty girl?" he asked as he grabbed her into a tight hug. Mia cringed when he did because she knew that Tre was probably watching everything. She was too scared to look over and see, so she focused her attention on the group of men in front of her. She pulled away from Cam and moved closer to her brother. Brandis looked kind of uncomfortable as well, and Mia knew that she was probably thinking the same thing. They both made small talk with Jabari and his friends for a while, before Brandis spoke up.

"Come walk with me to the bathroom Mia," Brandis requested. That was perfect timing because Camden was being too touchy feely. He was staring at Mia like she was his favorite candy and he kept trying to hug her. Mia kept pushing him away, but that didn't stop him from doing it again. Some niggas were really pathetic. Cam had a girl, but that never stopped him from doing him. Some of his girlfriend's people could have been there and he was trying to mess with Mia.

"Girl, I'm so happy that you pulled me away from his ass. That nigga can't keep his hands to himself for nothing," Mia complained.

"Yeah bitch, Tank was watching you the whole time. That's why I wanted you to walk away," Brandis replied while they walked towards the bathroom. Before they had a chance to go in, someone grabbed Mia's arm to stop her.

"How you doing?" an unfamiliar male asked while smiling down at her. He was tall with a low-cut fade and a pretty smile. He looked good as hell, but his timing was all wrong.

"Do I know you?" Mia asked the dirty-red complexioned cutie who wanted her attention.

"No, not yet," he flirted with a smile.

"Okay, so why are you touching me?" she snapped in aggravation. He immediately let her arm go and raised his hands in surrender. Mia rolled her eyes and continued on her way. They had a long line in the bathroom, but they didn't need to use it anyway. It was only a distraction for them to get away for a few minutes.

"Damn he was cute," Brandis said once they were away from Mia's admirer.

"He was, but I don't need Tre to see nothing else. He's probably already pissed about Cam," Mia replied.

"He kept looking at you, so I know he saw everything. Let's just stay in here for a few minutes and then we can go look for Tiara," Brandis suggested.

"Let me call and see exactly where she's at. I didn't think that this many people would be here," Lamia said while dialing's Tiara's number.

"Hey sis," Tiara answered on the third ring.

"Hey, where are you?" Mia asked.

"I'm standing by the front door with my cousins. Jabari said that you were looking for me, but I didn't see you anywhere. We went outside looking for you too."

"Okay, I'm in the bathroom, but stay where you are. I'll come to you so we don't keep missing each other," Mia suggested.

"Okay," Tiara said before disconnecting the call.

"She's standing by the front door. Let's go over there," Mia relayed to Brandis.

When they exited the bathroom, Mia was happy to see that the dude who tried to talk to her earlier was no longer standing there. She scanned the room and saw him standing against the wall talking to her brother's best friend, LJ.

"Mia, look," Brandis said, calling her attention to something across the room. She got heated when she saw Rainey and London standing there talking to Tre and Duke. Tre was smiling hard while London whispered something in his ear. He locked eyes with Mia, but he turned his head and kept right on talking and smiling in London's face.

"Oh okay," Mia retorted. "I guess we're free to do what we want to do now. In that case I need to stop turning all these niggas down and do me." Instead of going to look for Tiara like she originally planned to, she headed in the direction of LJ and her cute secret admirer.

"Mia, please don't go over there. You know Tank is going to act a fool up in here," Brandis pleaded nervously.

"Fuck Tank!" Mia spat right before she walked over to LJ. "Where's Jabari?" she asked her brother's friend just to make small talk.

"I think he went out front to smoke," LJ replied. The cutie who was trying to flirt with her earlier smiled at her and to his surprise, she smiled back.

"Damn, I got a smile," he said clapping his hands playfully. "You almost bit my head off when I touched you a few minutes ago."

"You shouldn't make a habit out of touching people that you don't know," Mia stated.

"You're right, my apologies for that," he replied. "What's your name?"

"Lamia," she responded. "What's yours?"

"Carrick, but I go by Ricky," he replied.

By then LJ had walked off to give them some privacy, but Brandis didn't know what to do. She hated to seem like she was being the third wheel, but she didn't know how Mia would feel if she walked away. She saw that Tre was looking right over where they were standing, but her girl wasn't paying attention. When Mia handed her new friend her phone to put his number in, Tre really looked like he was about to go off.

"Brandis!" Tre yelled while motioning her over to him. She looked at Mia to get the okay before she just walked off and left her. When Mia nodded her head saying that it was cool, Brandis walked off and headed in Tre's direction.

"What's up Tank?" Brandis asked when she walked up to him.

"What kind of fucking games is your friend playing?" he asked angrily.

"Please don't put me in the middle of y'all mess. I don't have anything to do with this," Brandis answered.

"You got a lot to do with it since that's your girl. She calls herself being funny by talking to that nigga in my face."

"But you were just talking to London in her face too," Brandis reminded him.

"I thought you just said that you didn't have anything to do with this."

"Well, you put me in it. Don't get mad with her when you were just doing the same thing. And where is that bitch London at anyway?" Brandis asked.

"I don't give a fuck about London, I'm not keeping tabs on that hoe," Tre barked. "You tell that bitch, Lamia that she got five minutes to meet me out back or I'm coming in here and drag her ass out.

I'm tired of her always playing with me like I'm some lil ass boy."

"Tank, just wait and talk to her later. Don't cause a scene at Jabari's party," Brandis begged.

"Fuck it, I'm going to get her ass myself," he replied as he headed in Mia's direction.

"No!" Brandis yelled grabbing his arm. "Okay, I'll tell her to meet you out back."

Tre looked at her skeptically, but he eventually gave in and stopped walking.

"Five minutes and I'm not playing," he said right before he disappeared towards the back doors of the building. Brandis rushed over to where Mia and her new friend were and interrupted their conversation.

"Excuse me, but I need to speak to Mia for a second," she said leading her friend away from Ricky.

"What's wrong?" Mia asked.

"Tank is trippin' and he wants you to meet him out back," Brandis replied.

"Girl, to hell with Tre. I'm done playing with his stupid ass."

"No Mia, I'm serious. He was coming over here to get you until I stopped him. He said if you're not out back in five minutes that he's coming in to drag you out. You know he's not playing, so you better dismiss your friend and go see what he wants."

"Okay, let me go tell Ricky that I'm leaving. Are you gonna be alright until I come back?" Mia asked.

"Yeah I'm good. I'm going to stand by Von until you're done. Just come get me," Brandis said walking away.

****

"You just keep taking me to play with, huh Mia?" Tre asked angrily. He and Mia had been arguing for the past five minutes and he was ready to knock her ass out at the moment. Her nonchalant attitude was really starting to piss him off.

"How am I playing with you? I figured that since you were smiling all up in London's face it was cool for me to mingle with other people too," Mia shrugged.

"So you thought it was cool for you to be all up in that nigga's face while I was standing not too far away from y'all?" Tre yelled.

"Yeah, just like you thought it was cool to be all up in London's face while I wasn't too far away from you. Then you looked right at me and kept talking to the bitch as if it was nothing. Do you, but don't think that I'm gonna be sitting around waiting until you're done."

"Man, fuck London! You talking like I want that bitch," Tre shouted.

"I really don't know who or what you want. Obviously, she was whispering something good in your ear the way you were smiling and shit."

"So you're mad that somebody else wants to be seen with me in public? Obviously you don't," Tre snapped.

"I'm so tired of having this same conversation with you Tre. You already know how I feel about that and I'm not going to keep repeating myself. I get that you want to have a relationship that can be out in the open and I don't blame you for that. I can't offer you that right now, so feel free to move on with somebody else who can. It's cool; you can be with London or whoever else you want to be with. I won't have any hard feelings and I promise that I won't interfere," Mia said as she attempted to walk away.

"So it's that easy for you to throw away a whole year of us being together Mia?" Tre asked sounding hurt. He pulled her back and turned her around to face him.

"I don't know what else you want from me Trevon. You knew what the deal was from the beginning, but you keep throwing the shit in my face every day. I'm tired of you always trying to

93

make me mad by entertaining the next bitch. I can't even get mad with London no more because you're playing the game right along with her."

"I'll admit that I was wrong for doing that, but you were wrong too Mia. And you're right; I did know how you felt from the beginning and I'm sorry for trippin'. I just don't want you to end what we have," Tre said honestly. He grabbed Mia around her waist and leaned down to kiss her lips. She hugged him back tightly, happy that they were able to resolve their minor issue.

"Okay, but I have a new rule and you need to follow it or we're going to have some problems," Mia announced. Tre pulled away and looked down at her like she was speaking a foreign language.

"I know you're not serious," he replied.

"Yes I am. I'm very serious."

"Okay, what's the rule?" He asked.

"As long as we're together, you can't talk or speak to London or Cheryl anymore. I don't care if they're at Von's house or in the streets. You're not allowed to speak to either of those bitches."

"I'm not allowed Mia?" Tre asked with raised brows.

"That's what I said. If I see you talking or speaking to them, we're going to have a problem," Mia promised.

"Okay, I won't say nothing to them anymore," Tre agreed. He couldn't believe that he was taking orders from a seventeen year old, but he would do anything to make Mia happy. It didn't matter whose feelings got hurt in the process.

Chapter 7

"Hey Jabari," Mia said when she answered the phone for her brother.

"What you doing Mia?" he asked.

"Nothing, I just got out of the shower and I'm getting dressed. Why, what's up?"

"I wanted you to take a ride with me. I'm going to take Tiara some lunch at work and I wanted you to come."

"Okay, just call me when you get downstairs," Mia said disconnecting the call. She hurried along and found something cute and comfortable to throw on, before Jabari came to get her. As soon as she was done, she walked out of her bedroom and found her brothers and sisters standing there waiting for her.

"Mia we're hungry and Moonie is still sleep," Anika spoke up.

"Tootie, you're the oldest, why didn't you fix them some cereal?" Mia asked her twelve-year-old sister.

"They didn't want any cereal. They want grits and eggs, but I can't cook hot food for them. Moonie said for us not to mess with her stove," Tootie replied. Mia was pissed as she stormed into

Moonie's room and turned on the lights. She was hoping to catch Dalvin's stupid ass in the bed with her so she could go off on both of them at the same time. Since her mother was in bed alone, that would have to wait for another time.

"Moonie wake up!" Mia yelled while shaking her mother hard. Moonie groaned a little, but she still didn't budge. Mia wasn't leaving her room until she was wide awake, so she continued to shake her and yell her name until she said something.

"What Mia, I can't even get no sleep in this damn house!" Moonie exclaimed sleepily.

"That's all the hell you do is sleep. Your kids are hungry and I'm getting ready to go. I'm getting tired of doing everything while you lay up in this bed and sleep all day. We have a house full of food, but it's not going to cook itself. I'm about five minutes away from packing all of my shit and leaving!" Mia yelled. She walked out and slammed the door before her mother even had a chance to respond. Without another word being said, she went straight to the kitchen and started fixing her siblings a hot breakfast.

"You fixing us some grits and eggs Mia?" Anika asked.

"Yeah, I'm fixing it. Go sit down until it's ready," Lamia replied.

"We want sausage too," Anika said.

"Okay, I got you. Go watch TV until I'm done." Mia got everything that she needed from the fridge and put a pot of water on to boil the grits. As soon as she started cracking the eggs in a bowl, Moonie walked in with her hair tied up and a pair of wrinkled pajamas on.

"Sorry Mia, I'll take it from here," she said as she gently took the cooking spoon from Lamia's hand.

"Did you even know that Mitch got them some tickets to the circus for next weekend?" Mia asked her mother. They'd been on her dresser for almost two weeks, but she had yet to say anything about them.

"No," Moonie replied in a low tone, as if she was talking to her mother instead of her daughter.

"They've been on your dresser for over a week now. If it's not too much, do you think you can skip the club Friday to make sure you take them next Saturday?"

"Okay, I will," Moonie yawned right as Jabari called Mia's phone.

"I'm leaving, call me if you need me," Mia said right before she walked out. Moonie never asked where she was going and it's been like that since she got old enough to dress herself. In Louisiana, you were considered an adult at seventeen years old, but Mia became a woman years ago, by no choice of her own. With a mother like Moonie, you had to learn to fend for yourself at an early age. She provided food, clothing and shelter, but you were on your own after that. "I'm coming out now," Mia said, answering the phone for her brother.

"What's up?" Jabari asked Mia when she got into his car.

"Same shit different day," she shrugged as he pulled off. "But about that party last week."

"That shit was the truth, huh?" Jabari asked.

"Hell yeah it was," Mia replied laughing. After her and Tre had their little talk outside, she was really able to have fun and enjoy the party. She and Brandis hung out with Tre and Duke for the rest of the night and had a blast. Tre avoided London all night until she finally got the hint and left him alone.

"I heard that nigga Ricky was trying to get at you, huh?"

"Yeah, but why you said it like that?" Mia asked.

"Like what? That's LJ's people, so I really don't know him like that. He's been cool the few times we hung out, but that's about all I can tell you," Jabari replied.

"Oh, we talked on the phone a few times and he seems cool," Mia said.

"Bet, but uh, back to the real reason for my visit. Do you have anything that you want to tell me?" Jabari asked out of the blue.

"About Ricky?" Mia questioned.

"About anything at all. You know we don't keep shit from each other Mia. You're one of my best friends and you can tell me anything," Jabari said while looking over at her.

"I know that and when I have something to say you'll be the first one to know," Mia insisted.

"So were you ever planning on telling me about you and Tank?" Jabari asked taking her by surprise. Mia just knew that she was hearing things, so she needed her brother to repeat what he'd just said.

"Huh?" she asked trying her best to play dumb.

"If you say huh that means you can hear me," Jabari said calling her out.

"Who told you?" Mia asked deciding to just come clean about everything. Only a few people knew and she was going to check whoever took it upon themselves to tell her brother her business.

"Nobody told me, I saw the shit with my own eyes the night of my party. I should have put it together a long time ago, but y'all did a damn good job of hiding it."

"What do you mean you saw it with your own eyes?" Mia wondered.

"I was in the back behind the dumpster smoking, when I saw you and Tank come out. I was about to come ask you what y'all were arguing about until I saw y'all start kissing. At first I thought the weed was playing tricks on me, but when it happened again I knew I wasn't trippin'," Jabari said.

"I told him that I smelled weed out there, but he told me I was being paranoid," Mia snickered.

"So how long have y'all been creepin'?"

"It's been like a year now."

"A whole year and you never thought to tell me about it Mia? I don't have to ask if Von knows since I'm almost positive that he doesn't."

"No, he doesn't know and please don't tell anybody Jabari, not even Tiara," Mia begged.

"I won't tell anybody, but I'm in my feelings that you didn't trust me enough to tell me yourself."

"I'm sorry Jabari, but I was scared to let anybody find out. I don't want it to get back to Von. He's going to be pissed if it does."

"I don't know why. It's not like you and Tank are related. Honestly, I think the nigga is too old for you, but you're grown. Even if I tell you to stay away from him, I know you won't. This is something else that I fault Moonie for. If she was paying more attention to you none of this would have happened."

"You can't blame Moonie for everything Jabari. I knew what I was doing when I laid down with Tre."

"You can kill all that noise about your sex life. I really ain't trying to hear it," Jabari said making Lamia laugh.

"But seriously Jabari, you don't like me being with Tre?" Mia asked.

"Tank is cool and I know for a fact that he's good to you. Even though it's only like a three or four year age difference between y'all, I just feel like he's too old for you. Louisiana law says you're grown, so what I say really doesn't matter. As long as you're good then all is right with the world as far as I'm concerned. Getting hurt is a part of life, but I still don't want to see it happen to you."

They continued their ride with Mia filling him in about everything that happened with her and Tre up until the night of the party. She could tell that he wasn't feeling the relationship, but there was really nothing that he could do. He didn't have a problem with Tre, but he was having a hard time getting past the age difference. Jabari's reaction to the situation really made her not want to tell Von. If her own brother wasn't feeling it then Von would probably be ten times worse. That was what scared Mia the most.

***

The following weekend, Mia and Brandis got a ride to Von's house with Duke. Brandis couldn't spend the night because her mama was in one of her moods, but she was able to get away for a little while. Rainey said she was coming over, but she was still at home packing clothes when Mia called her. Von told them to leave some things at his house for when they came over and Mia did just that. Tre took her shopping and she had everything she needed at Von's house. Rainey always thought somebody was trying to take her shit, so she declined the offer.

"Damn, what's going on in there?" Duke said looking over at Mia.

As soon as the three of them walked up to the door, they heard Von yelling at somebody, but none of them knew whom he was talking to. Mia took her key from her purse and opened the door just so she could see. Von's voiced boomed even louder when they entered the house and Mia wondered what was going on.

"How can you be so fucking stupid?" Von yelled at Tre while he sat at the kitchen table with his head hung low. "I bust my ass to make sure you're straight and this is the fucking thanks I get? I lost eight years of my life to prison behind this same stupid shit. Even though I tried to give you whatever you wanted, you still couldn't keep your dumb ass out of jail. If this is the life that you want to live, let me know now so I can be done with your ass. I'm not doing the jail thing with you no more Tank, and I mean that shit."

Mia was shocked to hear Von going off on Tre like that. She'd heard Von fuss at him more times than she could count, but never to that extent. He was damn near foaming from the mouth he was so mad. He had beads of sweat forming on his forehead and his fists were pounding the table with every word he spoke.

"Sorry Von," Mia said lowly as she and Brandis walked through the kitchen followed closely by Duke. They all went into the spare bedroom and waited while Von continued his verbal assassination. About ten minutes passed before they heard the front door slam. Tre walked into the bedroom and flopped down on the bed next to Mia. They all sat around in silence for a while, all seemingly lost in their own thoughts. When Tre pulled Mia close to him and hugged her from behind, Duke and Brandis got the picture and left them alone.

"What happened?" Mia asked as soon as they were alone.

"Stupid ass Ro gave Von some money that he owed me for fronting him some weed. Von found out that I'm selling again and you know how he feels about that," Tre responded.

"What do you mean selling again? You never stopped," Mia replied.

"You know that, but Von doesn't have to."

"I really don't understand why you're still hustling though. Von makes sure you have more money than you'll ever need with all the rental property he got for you. You own an entire apartment building Tre."

"But that's just it Mia, Von got that for me. I didn't work for that shit, it was handed to me. I feel like a child depending on his daddy to take care of him. At least when I hustle I know that's money that I worked hard to get."

"You are so stupid. All of the shit is in your name Tre. It doesn't matter how you got, it's yours. You sound so selfish right now. You know how many twenty-one year olds would be happy to take your place?" Mia said.

"I know and I'm chillin' out after I get rid of this last stash. I just want to make sure we're straight Mia. I don't want you to want for anything and I don't want you asking nobody else for nothing either."

"You make enough money legally to make that happen. Besides, if you're in jail I'll have to depend on somebody else anyway. You're really not making sense right now."

"Shut up and get naked," he said while climbing on top of her.

"No Tre, you don't know where Von went and he might be coming right back," Mia objected.

"You got to give me a quickie or something Mia, please," Tre begged.

"Okay, lay down so I can get on top to make sure it's quick," Mia laughed.

"Bet," Tre said excitedly as he jumped up and locked the door. He grabbed Mia and started taking off her clothes as soon as he got back to the bed. Once they were both naked, he pulled her on top of him and was about to enter her before she stopped him.

"Don't play with me Tre," Mia said looking down at him.

"Damn Mia, why can't we ever have sex without me licking on you first?" Tre complained while pulling her up to sit her on his face.

"Because I said so," Mia moaned while grinding all over his face. He was complaining, but he seemed to be enjoying it more than she was. He was moaning just as much as her, and she was the one being pleasured. He had a firm grip on Mia's hips and she couldn't move even if she wanted to.

She rode the wave for all of ten minutes before the sensation became too much for her to handle.

"Okay Tre, let me up," Mia panted just as her legs started to shake uncontrollably. Tre ignored her, so she pried his hands from around her hips and lifted up.

"You are so damn backwards girl. You always want your pussy in my mouth, but you can't take it when I give you what you ask for," Tre laughed.

"Shut up," Mia said as she slid her body down and straddled him. She lifted up just enough for him to enter her, before sliding right back down. Tre tried to make her go down further, but he would probably rip her open if she did. Once Mia's body adjusted to his size, she put her hands on his chest and started bouncing on him, just like he showed her a while ago. He taught her well and she knew just what he liked.

"Damn Mia," Tre moaned while throwing his head back and closing his eyes. He put his hands behind his head and let Mia take him into another world. "Don't go too fast, slow down."

"No Tre, you said a quickie remember?" Mia reminded him. It felt so good that he wasn't trying to complain. After a few minutes of lying flat on his back, Tre sat up on his elbows and locked eyes with Mia. When they first hooked up she was shy and would get mad when he did that. Now that she was familiar with him, she looked right back at him while she did her thing.

"You working hard for your birthday gift, huh?" Tre joked while smacking Mia's ass hard. Her birthday was two weeks before she went back to school and she'd been begging him to take her to Miami.

"Yep and I better get what I want too," Mia said while never missing a beat. She didn't even have to ask twice. She was getting her trip to Miami and whatever else she wanted. Tre was about to tell her that until Brandis' voice stopped him.

"Von just pulled up y'all," she yelled frantically.

"Man fuck!" Tre cursed when Mia jumped up from the bed. "This is that bullshit that I be talking about Mia. We need to start getting a room again or I need my own spot."

Tre used to get rooms for them at least twice a week, but they stopped when Von started spending nights at Cheryl's house. They had the whole place to themselves then, so there was no need to spend money if they didn't have to. Since Von started kicking it with Tanya again, he started staying at home more often. Tanya and Duke lived in a nice big house in Gretna, but she would spend nights at their house sometimes too.

"I'm sorry baby," Mia said as she gathered her clothes and raced to the bathroom.

"Sorry my ass, you owe me Mia. I don't give a damn what time Von goes to sleep, you better be up and ready," Tre said as he followed right behind her.

He snatched the towel from her hands and put soap and warm water on it. Mia smiled while he leaned down and cleaned her up. Once he was done, she got dressed while he freshened himself up. When they were both dressed, Tre peeped out into the hall to make sure the coast was clear. He didn't see anybody so he hurried to his room while Mia went to the front of the house. She noticed that Von had lots of different Chinese foods spread out on the counter, so that explained where he went. Duke and Brandis were already digging in and Mia was ready to join them.

"I'm sorry about earlier y'all," Von apologized. "I try not to let too many things upset me, but that boy is trying to send me to an early grave."

"You don't have to apologize Von, this is your house," Mia replied right as the doorbell rang.

"That's probably Cheryl," Von said causing Mia to roll her eyes. He walked away to answer the door while Mia grabbed a plate and started fixing her food. When London and Cheryl walked into the kitchen, she rolled her eyes again and stared eating.

"Rainey is pulling up," Von announced. As soon as the words left his mouth, she came strutting in the house with a Gucci overnight bag in her hands.

"Friend, I love that bag. I got to get me one of those," London gushed while feeling the material on Rainey's bag. Mia didn't miss how close the two of them seemed and London calling Rainey friend didn't go unnoticed either.

"Thanks chick," Rainey replied. "My mama and step daddy got it for me when they went to New York last month."

"Y'all come get something to eat while it's hot," Von said. "Duke, go get your boy and tell him to come eat. I'm pissed with the nigga, but I'm not trying to starve him."

Duke walked off towards Tre's room while Cheryl, London and Rainey fixed their food. By the time Duke and Tre came back to the kitchen, Mia and Brandis were done eating, but they sat at the island and talked to Von. As soon as Tre entered the room, he started fixing his food like he was in a hurry.

"Hey Tank, I haven't seen you in a while," London said with a smile. She was waiting for him to respond, but he never said anything. Even though she was talking loud enough for everyone to hear, she figured that maybe he didn't hear her.

"You heard me Tank? You've been missing in action lately, huh?" London spoke up again. Tre looked over at Mia, but again he didn't acknowledge London or answer her question.

"Are you alright Tank?" Cheryl asked trying to save her daughter from being embarrassed any further. He and London usually got along just fine, so she didn't know the reason behind the silent treatment that he was giving her. She knew for a fact that they talked on the phone sometimes, but he was acting strange at the moment. But just like he'd done to her daughter, Tre was ignoring her too. Cheryl didn't know what the problem was, so she shut up and left it alone. It didn't help much that Mia and Brandis were laughing like some damn fools.

"What the hell is wrong with you boy?" Von yelled to his son.

"Nothing is wrong with me," Tre snapped, as he grabbed his plate and walked down the hall to his room and slammed the door.

"I'm sorry about that y'all. That nigga is still heated because I got on his ass about something earlier," Von said apologetically.

"I knew something had to be wrong. That's not like him at all," Cheryl replied.

"And what are y'all crazy asses laughing at?" Von asked Mia and Brandis.

"Nothing," Mia laughed as she stood up from her seat. "Let's go check on your boy Duke."

111

Brandis followed her friend and Duke down the hall and into Tre's bedroom.

"Nigga, what the fuck was that all about?" Duke asked with a puzzled look on his face.

Tre cut his eyes over at Mia and shook his head.

"Ask her what it was about. That shit was so embarrassing. Got me standing there looking like a fucking retard," Tre fumed.

"Hold up nigga, nobody put a gun to your head and made you do a damn thing," Mia said seriously. "If it's that serious for you to hold a conversation with that hoe then go right ahead and do it."

"Don't start that shit Mia. I did what you told me to do, so you don't have a reason to be mad," Tre replied.

"Whatever nigga," Mia snapped with her arms folded across her chest.

"Come in the bathroom and let me talk to right quick," Tre requested pulling Mia by the hand. "Lock that door for me Duke."

"What?" Mia flippantly replied as soon as Tre closed the bathroom door.

"What's with the attitude?"

"I don't have an attitude. That's you getting mad because you couldn't speak to your bitch and her mama."

"Don't do that Mia. I'm not mad, but I know Von is probably looking at me like I'm crazy."

"Not really, he thinks you're pissed about the conversation that y'all had earlier," Mia said.

"That wasn't a conversation. That nigga straight went off on me. But that's what I wanted to talk to you about. Duke asked me if I wanted to chill by his house for a few days until the smoke clears here. I told him that I thought it was a good idea, but I wanted to run it by you first."

"I'm cool with it. You and Von might need a few days apart," Mia laughed. "Oh, and I have something to tell you too."

"What?" Tre question.

"Jabari knows about us," Mia confessed.

"How? I know you didn't tell him."

"No, he said he saw us outside kissing the night of his party. Remember when I told you I smelled weed?" Mia laughed.

"His ass was out there smoking," Tre said more as a statement than a question.

"Yep," Mia replied.

"I'm sorry baby," Tre said pulling her to him. "I should have waited until we left to talk to you."

"It's cool, he won't tell anybody," Mia shrugged. They stood around in the bathroom hugging and talking, until Brandis announced that her and Duke were about to go. Mia and Tre walked them out before going to their separate rooms and waiting for Von to fall asleep.

Chapter 8

"Paige, stop acting like a rookie and do it right!" Tre yelled angrily.

He was standing up against the dresser while she kneeled down in front of him with his dick in her wet mouth. She kept twirling her tongue around the head teasing him, and he was getting pissed off. He'd been at her house for the past three days, even though Mia thought he was at Duke's. He kept his routine the same and he still called her every day just like always. He even picked her up the day before and took her shopping and out to eat, to make sure that she didn't get suspicious. Paige bitched the whole time he was gone because he turned his phone off. He really didn't care just as long as Mia was happy.

"Mia really must not know how to suck dick, huh?" Paige asked looking up at him.

"Man, fuck it! Get up so I can get the hell up out of here," Tre said in aggravation.

He really didn't have time to play with her right now. She was always worrying about what Mia did or didn't do. Truth be told, Lamia had never given him oral sex and that was cool with him. He really didn't need her to as long as Paige and a few others freaks were willing to do it for him. Although Paige's head game was the best, he could have done without all the games that she kept playing. Her kids were outside in the yard and he needed her to hurry up and finish before they came back in.

"Stop whining and let me do this," Paige said right as she took him all the way to the back of her throat. Tre closed his eyes and tightly gripped her shoulder-length bob with both hands. He was hoping that she didn't want him to fuck her because he wasn't in the mood for all that. They'd only had sex twice since he'd been there, but he could do without it. She pulled out all the tricks that had him hooked when he was younger, but he still wasn't interested. He was sixteen when he first hooked up with Paige and nobody could tell him that she didn't have the best pussy in the world. Then he hooked up with Mia and found out that everything he thought about Paige was a lie. She was loose and worn out, but he didn't know that until he saw how tight Mia was and still is. She was the first virgin that he'd ever been with and there was no turning back after that. Paige was a cute girl with her light brown complexion, full pouty lips and big brown eyes. She still had a nice figure even though she had three kids. She just wasn't Mia.

"Shit," Tre hissed as Paige tried to suck the life out of him. He was all the way to the back of her throat and she didn't gag or flinch one time. She was working her magic on him and he was seriously debating if he wanted to stay another night with her. He was supposed to be going by Duke's for a few days before going back home, but she was about to make him change his mind. When he felt himself about to cum, he tapped Paige on her shoulder trying to get her to move, but she kept going. A few seconds later, he was releasing everything he had down her throat and she took it all in like a pro. Tre knew that wasn't her first time swallowing because she seemed too comfortable with doing it. That was her first time doing it to him and she had him spent. He was too weak to continue standing, so he slid down to the carpeted floor and tried to catch his breath.

"Tank," Paige said in her soft voice.

"What's up?" he asked with his eyes shut tight.

"Don't you think it's about time that you returned the favor?" Paige asked making his eyes pop wide open. He pulled up his boxers and his pants before he sat up and rested his back against her dresser. He knew what she was talking about, but it wasn't happening.

"Man, I already told you that I don't eat no pussy," he lied while looking her right in the eyes.

Mia was the first and only female that had that privilege and hopefully, she would be the last. He couldn't get with how some niggas went around licking on every female they sexed. He wasn't about that life at all. Even if he were Paige wouldn't know about it. She got around too much for him to put his mouth anywhere on her, even her lips.

"You need to stop acting like a lil ass boy. You're probably the only nigga I know that don't go down on his girl," Paige yelled angrily.

"You might want to get on the phone and holler at one of them other dudes then. I already told you that I'm not that nigga. And you ain't my girl so why would I put my mouth on you anyway?" he laughed.

"Oh, so now I'm not your girl? You weren't saying that shit a minute ago when I had my mouth all over you."

"It's not like I forced you to, that was your choice. You could have said no, but a nigga happy as hell that you didn't," Tre chuckled as he stood to his feet.

"I don't see what's so funny. I'm tired of you coming here only when it's convenient for you. Mia ain't your girl either, but you spend more time with her than anybody. I'm sure that's who you were with all day yesterday when you turned your phone off."

"I can't remember one time that Mia has mentioned your name other than when she got into it with your nieces. I don't understand why you always bring her name up every time you open your mouth."

"It's all good, tell your bitch that we'll be seeing each other real soon," Paige said nodding her head.

"That's cool, but I already told you how I feel about that. Just know that you and your people can get it too," Tre warned.

"But you don't mess with her though," Paige yelled as she followed him out of her bedroom.

"How do you let a seventeen year old have you going crazy like this?" Tre asked.

"I'm not going crazy; I just want you to be honest with me."

"And then what?" Tre questioned. "If I did tell you that I was messing with her what could you do about it?"

"So you're finally admitting to it?" Paige said sounding hurt.

"I'm not admitting to shit. I'm just saying that if I was dealing with her there's not a damn thing that you could do about it," Tre replied.

"Okay," Paige smirked right as he walked out of her front door and slammed it shut.

***

"Mia, promise me that you won't tell Tank or Duke what I'm about to tell you," Brandis begged her best friend. Mia was sitting on her bedroom floor eating ice cream, when Brandis came over and said that she had something to tell her. Just by the look on her friends face she knew that it wasn't good, so she braced herself for whatever she was about to hear.

"I promise I won't say anything Brandis. You know we don't even get down like that. Whatever you say won't go any further than this room," Mia swore.

"Okay, so me and Duke were on our way to the movies last night when Tank called him," Brandis started.

"I'm listening," Mia said encouraging her to go on.

"Well, apparently he's been spending nights by Paige's and not by Duke's like he lied and said. Duke's volume on his phone was loud as hell and I heard everything. Tank was telling him that he would probably come by his house today or tomorrow because Paige was starting to get on his nerves. I tried calling you last night, but you didn't answer," Brandis informed her.

Mia knew that what her friend had to say was bad, but she didn't expect to hear that. Tre had been calling her non-stop every day since he'd been gone. They'd even gone shopping and out to eat one day, and to the movies the next. He didn't switch up on her at all, so she probably would have never figured it out. He was really doing the damn thing and Mia was pissed. She was also hurt and her appetite had vanished just that fast. She put the lid back on her ice cream and slid it away from her.

"I can't even front and say I don't care because my feelings are really hurt. But what I won't do is sit back and let a nigga dog me out. I don't give a fuck how much I love him. One thing Moonie taught me is that what one man won't do another one damn sure will. It's all good though. I hope he's planning on making it work with Paige because I'm done with his ass," Mia promised.

"I know you're going to tell him that you know, but please don't tell him that it came from me."

"C'mon now Brandis, you know I would never do that to you. He doesn't need to know where I got it from. All that matters is I know," Mia replied.

"So what are you going to do?" Brandis asked.

"Honestly, after shedding a few tears I'll have no choice but to pick myself up move and on. I told him from the start that I was cool if he wanted to do him. He claimed he was good, but obviously, he wasn't good enough. The thing that kills me with Tre is he wants to be with other people, but he wants me to remain faithful to him. I don't want him to get me being young confused with me being dumb. I talk to Ricky on the phone almost every day, but I keep turning him down every time he wants to take me somewhere. Here I am respecting this nigga and he was pretty much saying fuck me," Mia said getting upset.

"Maybe you need to take Ricky up on his offer," Brandis suggested.

"There ain't no maybe about it. I'm about to let this nigga see that one monkey don't stop no show. He had his fun and now it's time for me to have mine," Mia replied.

"I just don't want you to get hurt Mia. You know how men are. It's cool for them to do dirt, but they can't handle it when we do it."

"I'm not worried about Tre. Whatever happens he bought it on himself. But enough about his dog ass, what's up with you and Duke? I didn't know y'all were messing around," Mia smiled.

"We're not really messing around. He just asked me to go to the movies with him last night. After seeing what's going on with you and Tank, I'm kind of scared to even go there with him," Brandis confessed.

"You don't have anything to be scared of, Duke is nothing like Tre. He's actually one of the good ones, if there is such a thing."

"He's sweet and I like talking to him. Maybe we'll take it slow and see where it goes from there. I know Rainey is going to die if we do hook up," Brandis laughed.

"Girl please, it's not like he wants her anyway. I'm starting to give her ass the side eye, right along with London and Cheryl. I don't care that she's cool with them, but she better not ever play with me. God sister or not I'll deal with her ass, too, if it ever comes down to it. Tre is already on my shit list and I don't mind adding a few more names to it," Mia said seriously.

"I know that's right," Brandis said agreeing with her girl. She was happy that her mama and little sisters weren't home because she knew that her friend was going to need her. Mia was being strong right now, but she knew the moment that she was alone, she would probably break down. She hated to be the one to bring Mia the bad news, but she couldn't keep her best friend in the dark, especially when she was being done wrong. Brandis really liked Tre, but it would be nothing for her to cut him off if she had to. If she had to make a choice then it was very simple. Mia was her best friend and she was riding with her until the wheels fell off.

Chapter 9

Tre was literally ready to snap. Aside from her cursing him out like a dog, he hadn't heard from Mia in almost two weeks. The day after he left from Paige's house, he called her to see if she wanted to go out to eat, but he got the surprise of his life when he did. She told him that she knew he'd been sleeping by Paige's house and she was done with him. He knew that Paige was probably the one who ratted him out, but he didn't have a way of proving it. That was the only way Mia could have found out where he was, but he couldn't ask Paige about it. She would lie if he did, so he would be wasting his time anyway. If he was never done with her trifling ass before, he was definitely done with her now. He stashed some stuff at her house from time to time and that would be the only reason that he ever went over there.

"I'm really trying not to act a fool, but Mia is really playing with me hard. I'm trying to see why Brandis and the rest of her girls are here, but she's not. Who the fuck is she with?" Tre asked Duke angrily. They were at the gym that sat right in the middle of The Court, watching a basketball game and it was packed. Mia and her girls never missed a game, but all of them were in attendance except for her. Tre came through on his bike just in case she showed up. He didn't want her to recognize his car and leave.

"I don't even know man. I know that Brandis has been talking to her though. She was at her house the other day when I called. Mia spoke to me and everything," Duke replied.

"Every time I go by Moonie's house they tell me that she's not home. I know she got her lil sisters and brothers lying for her, but it's all good."

"She hasn't been coming by Von's house either?" Duke asked.

"Y ou already know she ain't coming over there if she's avoiding me. He's been talking to her though. She told him some lame ass lie about her spending time at home with her brothers and sisters. You know he believes everything she says. She ignores my calls, but she answered when I called from Von's phone. As soon as I started talking she hung up on me," Tre said shaking his head.

"Damn, Mia ain't playing with your ass," Duke laughed. "What about Jabari? He knows what's up with y'all now. Maybe you should see if he knows something."

"I went by his house too. He told me that she had just left with Tiara right before I pulled up. I chilled over there for a while trying to see if she was coming right back, but I ended up leaving after a while. It ain't like she's hiding, she's just avoiding me. Her routine is the same except for her coming by Von's. She knows she'll have to face me if she comes over there."

"But who is she hanging with like that? It's rare that you see her and Brandis apart," Duke observed.

"That's what the fuck I want to know," Tre said getting mad all over again. "I'm going swing by Moonie's again before I go home. Hit me up later so we can hook up."

"Alright, and don't get yourself in no trouble bruh," Duke said dapping his friend off.

Tre got on his bike and drove the short distance to Mia's building. It was dark outside, so he knew that her sisters and brothers were already in for the night. She had them trained to be inside at a certain time and they always listened. He saw Moonie's car in her assigned spot, so that was a good sign that maybe Mia was at home. Tre parked his bike on the side of the building and hiked up the stairs to the apartment. He knocked on the door and waited for someone to answer. When he heard the locks being undone without anyone asking who it was, he knew that it had to be one of the younger kids. When the door opened and he saw Anika standing on the other side of it, he really wasn't surprised. She was bad as hell and basically did whatever she wanted to do. She barely listened to Moonie, but she didn't play with Mia.

"Where is Mia, Anika?" Tre asked the cute brown-skinned little girl who was staring up at him. Just by looking at her, you would never know that she was a mess with a mouth like a grown woman.

"She's not here, she's with her boyfriend," Anika said making his heart beat rapidly in his chest.

"What boyfriend?" Tre questioned angrily.

"I don't know his name. He got a black truck like Moonie's," Anika informed him.

"What the hell I tell you about opening my door Anika? Who is that?" Moonie yelled.

"Don't holler at me, that's Tank," Anika flippantly replied as she walked away. Instead of Moonie correcting her, she rolled her eyes and walked over to the door.

"What's up Tank?" she smiled while opening the door wider for him to come in. She had on her clubbing clothes, so he knew that she was about to hit the streets.

"Nothing, I was looking for Mia."

"She left with her lil friend, but she should be back in a minute. She's watching the kids for me and she told me that she would be back around eight or nine," Moonie replied.

"What lil friend?" Tre asked.

"Some nigga named Ricky. I told her that she better let you and Von meet him to see if y'all approve or not," Moonie laughed. "You can stay here and wait for her if you want to."

"Yeah I'll do that. You can leave if you have somewhere to be. I'll keep an eye on them until Mia gets back," he offered. Moonie's eyes lit up at the possibility of being able to leave earlier.

"Are you sure Tank?" she asked just to be sure. She was already grabbing her keys off of the counter before he even answered her.

"Yeah I'm sure. I'll chill and watch a movie or something until she gets back."

"Okay cool. They already ate and had their baths. The boys are in the room playing their game and Tootie is watching TV. This thing here is the only one that you'll probably have to worry about," she said pointing to Anika.

Moonie grabbed her purse and almost ran out of the door, locking it behind her. Tre looked around at the apartment and nodded his head in admiration. Moonie almost had it looking like a museum up in there it was so nice. She didn't have a job, but somebody must have been breaking some serious bread with her. More than likely that someone was Dalvin.

"You know Mia's boyfriend Tank?" Anika asked breaking the silence.

"Nope," he replied while flipping through the channels on the TV with the remote.

"You don't like him?"

"I don't know who her boyfriend is. Has he been over here before?"

"He never came in here, but he picks Mia up from in front of the building in a black truck," Anika revealed. Tre just nodded his head as Anika told him everything that she knew about Mia's new man. He asked a few questions, but she volunteered everything else. Before long, it was after ten o'clock and Mia still wasn't home. Tre was happy that Anika had finally gone to sleep though. Tootie told him that he could lay her in the bed and he was happy to do it. She was beneficial with the info that she gave him, but she talked him half to death. Once he made sure that all of the kids were straight, he watched TV and waited for Mia to come home. He would have waited in her bedroom, but she always kept her door locked. Thankfully, he didn't have to wait long. Tre heard what he thought was arguing downstairs and he got up to look out of the front window. He didn't see anybody, but he was just in time to see a black Escalade pull up just like the one Anika said Mia's so-called boyfriend had. A few minutes passed before anybody got out, and Tre was ready to go down there and see just who was behind the wheel. Just as he'd made up his mind to go, the driver's side door opened and a dude jumped out of the truck. He walked around to the passenger's side and opened the door for Mia. It was then that Tre realized who it was. The same dude that Mia was talking to at the party was the one who she was spending time with now. Tre was pissed, but he decided to wait it out. He watched as they embraced for a while before he walked Mia to the door and he left. Tre turned the TV off and sat in the dark, waiting for her to open the door.

***

"I know she didn't leave them in here alone just so she could go out," Mia muttered as she fumbled around in her purse looking for her house keys.

When she pulled up, she noticed that Moonie's truck wasn't in the driveway like it usually was. Maybe the kids were with Jabari, but she didn't know for sure. She was supposed to be home hours ago to keep them, but she was enjoying herself too much to rush. Ricky had taken her to a water park in Mississippi and she felt like a big ass kid playing on all the rides. She knew that Moonie would be mad that she was late, but she really didn't care. She could stand a few days away from the club anyway. Mia opened the door to the darkened living room and felt against the wall for the light switch. As soon as she turned it on, she was scared half to death by Tre's angry voice.

"So how long have you been messing with that nigga Mia?" he asked as he stood from the sofa and walked over to her.

"What the hell are you doing in here Trevon? You almost made me piss on myself," Mia yelled while grabbing her chest. He was the last person that she wanted to see. She'd been going out of her way for almost two weeks to make sure she didn't.

"That's your boyfriend Mia? That's damn sure what your family seems to think."

"I don't have a boyfriend, but I'm taking applications," Mia said smartly.

"You think that shit is funny?" he yelled getting in her face.

"Am I smiling nigga? What I do is no longer your concern. Get your life and stay out of mine."

"So running to another nigga is how you deal with problems? We were supposed to sit down and talk about this shit Mia. You really need to grow the fuck up," Tre snapped.

"What's there to talk about? I told you that I was done and the conversation was over after that. I also told you to make it work with Paige or move on and find you somebody new," Mia said as she unlocked the door and stepped into her bedroom.

"I don't want Paige or anybody else and I wish you stop saying that."

"Obviously you do. For you to lie to me just to spend time with her is all the proof that I need. It was fun while it lasted, but I'm done," Mia promised.

"Let's just sit down and talk about this Mia, please," Tre begged.

"We're talking right now Tre. The problem is that I'm not telling you what you want to hear."

"Baby I'm sorry. Just give me another chance to get it right. I promise I won't do anything to mess it up this time," he pleaded. "I do one stupid thing and you just give up on me like this?"

"One?" Mia shouted. "You keep doing stupid shit because I keep forgiving you. You're always taking my kindness for weakness and ain't nothing weak about me. You can keep your promises and your fake ass tears this time around. It's over and I mean it."

"Mia please, I'll do whatever you want me to do. Just don't break up with me," Tre pleaded while pulling her closer to him.

"No Tre. Honestly, I don't feel like you deserve me. Even though nobody really knew that we were together, I still remained faithful to you. I always took your feelings into consideration even though you never gave a damn about mine. It's not even worth it," Mia answered.

"Don't say that Mia. You can't tell me that you don't know how much I love you."

"As much as I hate to admit it, I love you too and probably always will. But sometimes love just isn't enough. Obviously, you didn't love me enough to keep your dick out of the next bitch. I'm tired Tre, let me walk you out, so I can take a shower and go to bed," Mia said as she led the way out of her bedroom.

She felt like crying, but she would never let him see her tears. Even though she'd been spending time with Ricky, Tre was all that she thought about. She would never let him know it, but she knew in her heart that she wasn't ready to completely end their relationship. She just had to let him know that she had other options just as well as he did. He couldn't keep thinking that his apologies were going to fix every problem they had. Mia wanted him to feel the same pain that she felt. Judging by the somber look on his face, she knew that he had.

"Can you at least answer my calls or text me back?" he asked just above a whisper.

"I don't know, I'll think about it," Mia said holding the front door open for him to walk out.

"C'mon Mia, at least give me that much. We used to talk all the time before we started messing around."

"I don't care about what happened before we hooked up. I said I'll think about it," Mia repeated. He tried to lean down to give her a kiss, but she turned her head the opposite way.

"I love you," Tre said right before he walked out of the front door. Mia locked the door behind him right as the tears started creeping from her eyes.

Chapter 10

"I must have really done something to piss you off. I can't even remember the last time I saw you," Von joked when Mia walked into the house with Rainey and Brandis. He hadn't seen her in three weeks and he had to call her to come over for a visit. Rainey had been over there every weekend, but it wasn't the same without his Mimi.

"Don't do me like that Von, you're making me feel bad," Mia pouted. She really did feel bad for making Von suffer for what Tre had done, but she just didn't want to see him. Von was used to seeing her at least once or twice a week, but almost a month had passed since her last visit. They talked on the phone all the time, but that wasn't good enough. She missed him and it was obvious that he missed her too. She was just hoping that she could continue to be strong once she saw Tre. Brandis' mama went out of town with her sisters and Moonie agreed to let her stay with them for the week. Mia was happy because her bestie would be spending the weekend at Von's house with her. That way she didn't have to be bothered with Rainey's disgusting ass all weekend.

"You should feel bad. When did I have to start calling you to come spend some time with me? I've been sitting in here bored for the past few weeks," he said laughing.

"Now that was a cheap shot Von. Me and London have been keeping you company every weekend," Rainey said sounding offended. Mia's head snapped around to face her upon hearing London's name. Since she hasn't been around for the past few weeks Tre was probably screwing London too. She didn't put anything past him anymore.

"I'm just joking Rainey. I'm used to both of y'all being here every weekend. London is cool, but she can't take the place of my baby. You are staying for the weekend right?" he asked while hugging Mia.

"Yeah I'm staying. I hope my stuff is still where I left it because I didn't bring anything," she replied.

"It's all there," Von replied. "We need to get a menu together for tonight. I need to go to the store and pick up a few things."

"You never cooked one time while I was here by myself. You kept filling me up with fast food," Rainey chuckled.

"I didn't have anything to cook," Von answered. "Tanya has been bringing food over here and I haven't gone to the store in a minute."

"Tanya needs to come over here now so we can discuss my birthday trip to Miami. She said she was coming and she better not change her mind," Mia chimed in.

135

Tanya promised that she would clear her schedule for the entire week to accompany them on their trip to Miami. She made sure to ask her months in advance, before Von tried to invite Cheryl or one of his other side bitches to come along. Tre was supposed to be making everything happen, but Mia wasn't looking forward to that since they were no longer together. Honestly, she wouldn't even be mad if he decided not to go with them. That's just how mad she was with him at the moment.

"Is your birthday coming up?" Von smirked.

"Very funny Von," Mia replied.

"We'll talk about that later, but what do y'all want to eat?" Von asked.

"Let's eat crab cakes and shrimp pasta," Mia suggested. Brandis was okay with the menu, but Rainey just had to be different.

"I don't want that. I want some barbecue shrimp with French bread," she argued.

"Okay," Mia agreed. "We can do that. I'm cool either way."

"I'll do both," Von said standing to his feet. "I'll get us some junk food for the weekend too since the weather is supposed to be bad."

He got his keys and wallet from his room and headed for the door, right as Tre and Duke walked in carrying a cake that Tanya sent over. Mia immediately turned her head when her eyes met with Tre's. She didn't speak to Duke either because it would have been too obvious and Von would have picked up on it.

"Where are you going?" Tre asked his father.

"I need to pick up a few things from the store so I can cook," he replied.

When they started talking, Mia used that as her opportunity to go into the spare bedroom where she slept. She wanted Brandis to come, but she could have done without Rainey following behind them. Mia knew that she and her God sister had to have a serious talk soon. They were drifting apart for some reason and she wanted to know why. Mia didn't care for London, but that didn't have anything to do with Rainey. She really didn't care that the two of them were friends, but she didn't want Rainey to feel like she had to choose a side. That was childish and Mia wasn't with that.

"Give me some gum Mia," Brandis requested right when they walked into the room.

"My girl is trying to make sure that breath is fresh for Duke," Mia laughed.

"I didn't know that you and Duke messed around Brandis," Rainey said trying hard not to sound as jealous as she was.

"Who said that we mess around?" Brandis asked.

Just then, the door to the room opened and Duke came strolling in. Brandis got butterflies in her stomach every time she saw him and she felt them fluttering right at the moment. Duke was a dark skinned cutie with neat dreads that he kept tied to the back of his head. He reminded Brandis of the rapper Young Buck, but he was a real sweetheart.

"What's up y'all?" Duke asked when he walked in. They all spoke back, but Rainey was a little extra as usual.

"What's up handsome?" she flirted just like always.

"Nothing much, I'm just coming to check on my future wife," he replied making Brandis blush.

"I thought you said y'all didn't mess around Brandis," Rainey said trying to be messy.

"No, I asked you who said that we mess around. Don't try to put words in my mouth and don't try to define what we have going on. That's nobody's business if we mess around or not," Brandis corrected.

"No need for the attitude," Rainey frowned.

"Okay that's enough. Just let it go," Duke whispered to Brandis.

Mia wanted to laugh so badly, but she held it all in. Rainey was always trying to come for Brandis and she was finally starting to stand up to her. Usually, Mia would come to her defense, but her girl seemed to have it covered this time. Rainey wanted Duke in the worst way and it was killing her that he wanted Brandis instead. In Rainey's mind, it would be perfect if she hooked up with Duke along with London and Tank. She knew that Tank was messing with Mia, but that was never going to work. They had to keep their relationship a secret and that had to be tiresome. Plus, she knew that Von wouldn't approve of them being together anyway. He looked at Mia like a daughter, so he would never be all right with her being with his only son.

"What's up?" Tre spoke when he walked into the bedroom.

Mia turned her head and played on her phone while everybody else spoke to him. She still wasn't answering his calls and they hadn't talked since he came to her house the weekend before. He tried calling from other numbers a few times, but she always hung up on him. She was afraid of giving in too easily, so staying away was the best thing for her to do. If Von wouldn't have called her to come over, she probably wouldn't be over there at all. She sat in the bed with her back up against the wall trying hard not to make eye contact with him. When Tre walked over to the bed and grabbed her phone, Mia was on her feet in a matter of seconds.

139

"Give me my phone Tre," she yelled as she tried to snatch it out of his hand. He held her back with his free hand while he scrolled through the messages between her and Ricky with his other. Mia seemed to be feeling her new friend and he didn't like that at all.

"So you ignore all of my calls and texts, but you run it on the phone with this nigga all day," Tre said angrily.

"Don't worry about me. You're with Paige now right?" Mia yelled.

"You know I'm not with that damn girl. I don't know why you would even say some shit like that," Tre fumed.

"I'm saying it because you were just fucking her a few weeks ago. Maybe you're fucking London now. I don't put anything past you," Mia implied as she continued to reach for her phone.

"London!" Tre shouted. "Thanks to you I don't even speak to the damn girl no more."

"We're not together anymore, so you're free to speak to anybody you want to."

"I'm going in the living room Mia," Brandis said. She was trying to give them some privacy even though they didn't ask for it.

"You don't have to leave Brandis. It ain't even like that between us no more," Mia noted.

"Don't do this to me Mia. I swear I haven't been doing nothing but sitting in this house for the past few weeks. Duke can vouch for me because he's been here most of the time with me. And Rainey can tell you that I haven't said one word to London the entire time she's been coming over here. Tell her Rainey," he said turning to face his other God sister.

"He's telling the truth Mia," Rainey said even though she wanted to stay out of it.

She could have killed him for putting her in the middle of their mess. In her opinion, Tre was stupid for begging Mia to be with him. He had plenty of women begging for his attention, including London. If Mia wanted to be stubborn then he needed to leave her alone and move on.

"I really don't care one way or the other," Mia said as she attempted to walk away. Tre grabbed her arm and dropped down to his knees right in front of her. He didn't care that his best friend and hers were right there looking. He knew that Rainey was probably looking at him crazy too, but he didn't care about that either. He was really in love with Mia and he couldn't let her go without giving it his all.

"This nigga is going crazy," Duke mumbled to himself. He wasn't against going after what you wanted, but he wasn't as bold as his boy was. Begging behind closed doors was one thing, but he didn't think he could do it in front of anybody.

"Tre get up, this is not funny," Mia said embarrassed by his over-the-top display of affection.

"I'm not trying to be funny Mia. I need you to know how serious I am about us being together. Baby I'm sorry. I swear I won't do anything to make you leave me again. Just give me a chance to prove myself. I don't even care about us telling Von anymore," Tre pleaded. Mia wanted to keep playing hard to get, but he was making it almost impossible. Brandis and Duke looked like they felt sorry for him and Rainey almost looked like she was mad.

"Tre just get up. This is not the time for you to be doing this while we have a room full of people."

"I don't care about any of that. Everybody in here knows how I feel about you. Just one more chance, Mia, and I promise I'll get it right this time," Tre continued to beg. Mia wanted to smile at him, but she kept her hard girl act going. She had to let him know that she wasn't playing. He needed to know that he could and would be replaced if he didn't do right by her.

"Get up so we can talk face to face like adults," Mia said making him smile.

"My nigga was on his Keith Sweat begging shit," Duke said causing everybody to laugh. He, Brandis and Rainey left out of the room and allowed Tre and Mia to talk.

142

"Before you start with a bunch of apologies, let me run a few things by you first," Mia stated as soon as she was alone with Tre.

She'd been thinking about what she wanted to say to him for the past few weeks, and she was happy to finally get a chance to say it. There was no way that they could continue being together if he wasn't willing to be faithful. She could have been doing the same thing, but she chose not to. In Mia's mind, it was simple. Either they do things the right way or they didn't do anything at all.

Chapter 11

"Man, Tae, don't have me coming over there for nothing. Your people better be ready to spend some damn money," Tre fussed on the phone with his cousin. They had one week left before their trip to Miami and he was trying to unload all of his product before he left. His first cousin, Talen, begged him to let her and her girls take it off of his hands, and he agreed. Tae and her girls were born to hustle and were just as hard as Tre and his boys.

"Cuz I got you," Tae swore to him. "Everybody got their money. We're just sitting around waiting on you to show up."

Tae lived in the same apartment complex as Tre's mother, Terri. He didn't go over that way too often because he really didn't like running into her. He and Terri really didn't have a relationship and he preferred to keep it that way. The only time he made it his business to visit is when his brother and sister were there. When Von went to jail years ago, Terri got with a man named Darren and had two kids with him. Tre actually liked Darren because he treated him better than his own mother did. Even when Terri had his kids, Darren was still good to him. Terri was a street runner just like Moonie, but she was even worse. She didn't care if there was food in the house or clean clothes on their backs. As long as she was able to do whatever she wanted to do, that was all that mattered. Darren came home from work many nights to a dirty house and empty freezer. He hung in there as long as he could until he finally got tired and left. He took his kids and moved out one day, leaving Tre at home all alone with Terri. Thankfully, Von was released a few months later and Terri packed Tre up and sent him to live with his father. Von wasn't home for a good twenty-four hours and Terri was handing Tre over to him. She didn't even know if Von had a place to stay or not, and she really didn't care. She was free of kids and that was all she ever wanted.

"Tank," Tae yelled causing Tre to abandon his thoughts temporarily. He'd completely zoned out and forgot that he was on the phone.

"I'm here," Tre replied. "I'm handling something right now, but I'll be there as soon as I get done." He hung up the phone and looked over at Mia. He was bracing himself for her mouth because he knew that he was about to hear it.

"I thought you said you were done after you got rid of that last stash," Mia said staring at him.

"I was Mia, but I'm spending a lot of money on your birthday gift and this trip to Miami. Then you go back to school in three weeks and that's more money that I have to spend."

"I thought this trip to Miami was my birthday gift. That was all that I asked you for. And you know that Moonie got me for school, so you don't have to worry about that."

"No, I got you for school. You're not sleeping with Moonie, you're sleeping with me. And you know I'm getting you something else for your birthday. The trip to Miami is just something extra," he clarified.

"I appreciate that Tre, but don't use me as an excuse to keep doing what you're doing. I'm good and I don't ask you for anything," Mia replied.

"You don't have to ask me for anything. I know what you need and I make sure I provide it for you."

"Yeah, but you know how Von feels about that. You have money Tre. I just don't get you sometimes," Mia complained.

"I'm really done after this. If Tae comes through and takes this load off of my hands, I'll be straight. With that money and what I already have saved, your gift and this trip will be paid for."

"Don't lie to me just to shut me up."

"I'm not lying to you. I'm done with it after this, I promise."

"Okay," Mia replied even though she didn't believe him.

"Man, what's taking them so damn long? I'm ready to go. We've been sitting here for over an hour and it's not even crowded in here," Tre complained. They were at the clinic waiting to be seen and his patience was wearing thin.

146

"That's because we walked in without an appointment. They have to see their appointments first. We can leave if you want to, but you know what the deal is," Mia threatened.

They'd been back together for two months and she still refused to have sex with him until he got tested again. She made him do it a while ago before he took her virginity, and he swore that he was never doing it again. He kept refusing thinking that she was going to give in, but she wasn't budging. They were going to Miami in a week, so he needed to get it done. The results would be back in three days and that was perfect for him. As bad as he wanted to leave, he knew that he couldn't.

"You must be crazy if you think I'm going to Miami for a whole week and don't get no pussy. I already got blue balls from you making me go without for two whole months," he fussed.

"That's all on you. If you would have done it when I first told you to we wouldn't even be here right now. You were the one who did wrong, not me," she reminded him.

"How do I know that? You and ole boy might have done something that you're not telling me about."

"Unlike you, I know how to say no. I've known you all my life and you still had to wait for months before you got it. What makes you think that I would give it up to a nigga that I've only known for a few weeks? Two of my friends caught

147

STDs from their boyfriends, but I promise you that I won't be number three. And just to ease your mind, I'll be happy to get tested right along with you. I don't have anything to hide," Mia replied.

"You don't have to do that. I believe you," Tre clarified.

"No, we're doing it together. I don't want there to be any doubts from either of us," Mia said.

Tre nodded his head, but it really didn't matter to him. He trusted her and he knew that she didn't sleep around. Mia was the only person that he'd never used protection with and he didn't want to start now. Although he used protection both times that he slept with Paige, he couldn't blame Mia for not believing him.

"Trevon Harris," the nurse called after they waited for about another thirty minutes.

Both Tre and Mia got up and followed her to the back. Mia inquired about being seen as well and was given the green light. They both gave blood, followed by a urine sample and cheek swab. The HIV results came back in a matter of minutes, but everything else would be in the mail a few days later. After a few minutes, they were done and ready to go.

"I told you that I was good," Tre said once they were back in the car.

"You're good on the big test, but we'll see about everything else," Mia replied.

"That's the most important one. You can be cured of everything else."

"And?" Mia spat. "Just because it's curable doesn't mean that I want it. You sound stupid."

"Why are you so mean, Mia?" he asked leaning over the seat to give her a kiss.

"Where are we going?" she asked him.

"I need to drop something off to Tae and pick up some money up from Ro. Are you coming with me?"

"Yeah, but you're still letting me use the car later right?" she asked.

She and Brandis made plans to hit up the mall before their trip to Miami. Von practically had to beg Brandis' mama to let her go. Sometimes Shelia could be a sweetheart and other times she acted like a bitter bitch. It was almost as if she hated to see Brandis have fun. Once Von assured her that Brandis was in good hands, she finally gave in and agreed to let her go.

"I might, all depends on what you give me for it," Tre teased.

"Forget it; I'll get a ride on my own. Don't get mad when another nigga be bringing me."

149

"Don't play with me Mia. You know I'm just messing with you. I told you that you could use it once I finish doing what I have to do," Tre promised. "Have you thought about what I asked you?"

"Yeah, I've been looking at some stuff online. I guess I never really thought about college until you mentioned it a few weeks ago. You know Moonie don't care about stuff like that, but I saw a few things that I might be interested in. Since math is my favorite subject, I've been leaning more towards accounting."

"That's what's up," Tre smiled making her smile in return. "We'll talk about it some more when we come back from Miami."

They talked for a while before stopping to get something to eat. Once they were full, Tre headed in the opposite direction to his cousin Tae's house. Mia decided to stay in the car while he went inside. Tae was cool, but her and her girlfriend kept a house full of people and somebody was always fighting. The police were bound to run up in there at any time and Mia was surprised that it hadn't happened yet. She watched the door intently for five whole minutes, until it opened up and Tre came back out. He was almost to the car when he was stopped by someone yelling his name. Mia looked up right as Terri approached her son. He kept walking and got in the car like he didn't even see her.

"Don't do that Tre. At least speak to her," Mia said.

"Speak to her for what? She ain't been worrying about me and she don't need to start now," he replied as he started the car.

"You better not pull off," Mia ordered right as Terri came up to his lowered window. She looked like the streets had worn her out. Her once beautiful face looked old and tired. She was still pretty, but it was no comparison to how she looked a few years ago.

"Hey Tank," Terri smiled. "Hey Mimi," she said speaking to Mia.

Mia spoke back, but Tre looked straight ahead. He couldn't stand his mother and Mia understood why. Just like Moonie, Terri was a club hopper and street runner too. Moonie made sure her kids were straight, but Terri just didn't give a damn. Tre was always saying that she gave him away like a stray dog and he couldn't just forgive her for that. He remembered going months without seeing or talking to her and that was hard on him. After a while, he gave up and really didn't care if he saw her or not. Von always told him that he needed to respect her as his mother, but he didn't feel the same way. She didn't act like a mother and he didn't feel that she should be treated as one. At least Moonie made sure that Mia's needs were met, but he couldn't say the same thing about Terri. He didn't have anything to say to her and he was ready to go. Of course, Mia had to make him do the right thing just as she always tried to do. When she pinched his arm, Tre turned his head to look at his mother.

"What's up Terri?" he spoke dryly.

"Nothing much, how have you been?" she asked him.

"I'm good, but did you need something?" Tre asked making Terri feel uncomfortable. She knew that they had a lot of issues, but he wouldn't talk to her long enough for them to be able to resolve anything.

"I tried calling you a few times last week, but you didn't answer. Your brother and sister don't answer when I call them either," she said sadly.

"I've been busy, but what's up?" Tre asked.

"I really wanted to do something with you and your brother and sister together. It's been a while since we spent any time with each other. Maybe we can all go out to dinner one day next week, my treat. You can come too Mia," Terri smiled.

"We're going to Miami next week for Mia's birthday," Tre replied.

"Okay, well call me when you get back and maybe we can plan something then. Happy birthday Mimi, have fun in Miami," Terri replied.

Mia thanked her, but Tre only nodded his head right before he pulled off and left her standing on the sidewalk. He hated when she called Mia the nickname that Von gave her. She and Mia weren't even cool like that.

"I feel so sorry for her," Mia said once they were gone.

"Don't do that Mia. As much as you get mad with Moonie, I never once tried to make you feel bad about it. I don't know why you feel sorry for her anyway. She didn't want her kids anymore and she got exactly what she asked for. What about how I felt when she gave me to Von and never called or came around to see about me? She's the one who decided that she didn't want to be a mother anymore. She was too busy chasing behind dick to give a fuck about her own kids," Tre yelled angrily.

Mia was shocked at how fast Tre's attitude had changed up. He was smiling and in a good mood before Terri approached him. She knew that he was hurting, so she decided not to reply to his sudden outburst. Usually she would be going off on him, but she knew that now was not the time. When Mia turned her head and looked out of the window, Tre felt bad for snapping at her like he did. It wasn't her fault that Terri ruined his day. It never failed. He could be in a good mood and his entire day would go to shit, once he laid eyes on the woman that gave birth to him. Even still, he couldn't stop himself from loving her. Maybe if she'd shown him some kind of regret or remorse, he would feel better.

"I'm sorry baby," Tre said while grabbing Mia's hand.

"It's okay," Mia smiled while squeezing his hand. "You know I understand if nobody else does."

Moonie had her faults, but she wasn't as bad as some other mothers. Mia couldn't remember a time that they didn't have food to eat. The bills were always paid on time or earlier and they had everything they needed and more. Moonie really didn't know how to be a good mother, but she was a great provider. Mia loved her for that if nothing else.

"When I pick up this money from Ro you can drop me off home and take the car," Tre said as they drove. He was out of product and once he got his money from Ro, he was straight. He would have more than enough to make sure that Mia enjoyed her birthday.

A few minutes later, Tre pulled up to the corner store where he, Ro and a few of their other friends usually hung out. He spotted Duke and Ro shooting dice while a few other people stood around and watched.

"I'm going in the store," Mia announced when the car came to a stop. She and Tre got out of the car at the same time and approached the group of men.

"What's up y'all?" Tre spoke.

"Damn Mia," Ro said loudly. "When you gon' let me sample all that ass."

Mia rolled her eyes at him and walked into the store.

"Man, I'm tired of telling you about playing with her like that. You go too damn far," Tre frowned angrily. "Let's do this business so I can go."

"You know I'm just fucking with her," Ro replied while placing a huge knot of money into Tre's hand.

"Yeah, but I keep telling you to chill out. Obviously she's not interested in talking to you," Tre said.

"I really don't understand why me flirting with Mia gets to you so bad. She's Duke's God sister too, but I don't see him acting like that behind her. You don't give a damn about what Rainey does and I know that for a fact. You make me think you want Mia for yourself," Ro commented.

"Don't try to compare me to the next nigga. I can't speak for Duke and nobody else. I keep telling you that you're too damn disrespectful and I ain't feeling that shit."

"You need to get out of your feelings and stop taking everything so personal. Mia is grown and she can handle herself. As much as you disrespect these hoes out here, you shouldn't have anything to say about what I do," Ro replied.

"She ain't none of these hoes out here though," Tre said growing angrier by the minute.

"Y'all chill out bruh," Duke said trying to calm the situation. "Ro you're wrong, so just take your lick and keep it moving. You do too much. You know somebody is always telling you about how you disrespect females."

"I do what the fuck I want!" Ro shouted. "I'm a grown ass man. If I want to flirt with Mia and any other bitch I see that's exactly what I'm gon' do."

"You got that bruh," Tre said calmly.

He wasn't the type to argue with another nigga and Ro was no exception. He liked to cause a scene and be the center of everyone's attention. If a crowd was around, that only intensified his already cocky attitude. Tre had been cool with him long enough to know that Ro lived for the spotlight.

"Are you done?" Mia asked as she walked out of the store and stood directly in front of Tre.

He saw Ro nudge one of his friends right before he walked over to them. Tre already knew that he was about to try to show off. He always wanted to make sure his boys watched whenever he did something stupid.

"Yeah I'm done," Tre said as he handed her the keys to drive. Mia said goodbye to Duke and was about to get into the car when Ro walked up and grabbed her arm.

"You not gon' tell me bye Mia?" he asked flirtatiously.

"Bye Ro," she snapped while pulling away from him.

"No, I want a hug," he said as he stepped up and pulled her body close to his. When he grabbed a handful of her ass, Mia pulled back and was ready to go off on him, but Tre beat her to it.

"You must think it's a game. I guess I have to make you respect my mind," Tre growled as he slammed his fist into Roland's face.

Ro stumbled from the impact of the first blow, especially since he didn't see it coming. He was shook for a minute, but he was swinging back as best as he could after being caught off guard. Everybody was yelling about how hard Tre's first lick was and that only made the situation worse. Ro was a known shit talker in the hood and he knew that he would never be able to live that down. Tre was getting the best of him and that wasn't a good look either.

"Tre stop!" Mia yelled while walking over to the brawl.

Duke pulled her back because they were in a full-blown mix. She would gotten hit for sure if she tried to break it up. Mia had never seen Tre fight before and he was in full beast mode at the moment. He and Ro were both tall, but Ro was no match for the jabs that Tre were throwing at him. He was flinging him around as if he weighted nothing at all. When Ro tripped and fell to the ground, Mia was petrified when she saw Tre start to stomp him. She started screaming for someone to break them up, but nobody moved. Even Ro's friends were stuck as they watched them go at it like a bunch of wild animals.

"Duke, go get him," Mia begged as she pushed him over to the two men. Duke didn't want to get involved, but Mia was going crazy. Even though Ro deserved to get his ass beat, he hated that she was out there to witness it.

"C'mon man," Duke said pulling Tre off of Ro.

Tre looked over at the frightened look on Mia's face and regret set in soon after. He hated to do Ro like that in front of her, but he couldn't help it. He warned him too many times, but he didn't listen. When he grabbed Mia's ass like he did, Tre snapped and tried to kill him with his bare hands. One of their other friends walked over to help Ro up and he started running his mouth as soon as he was back on his feet.

"Nigga you a hoe," Ro yelled with blood dripping from his mouth and nose. "You had to sneak me just to win the fight."

"Let's go another round then nigga," Tre requested. "You already know you can't handle me."

"Tre no, let's just go," Mia begged. She grabbed his arm and pulled him towards the car.

"You act like you fucking Mia or something. If that's the case, share her like you share all of your other bitches. Nigga, I already know how you do it. Don't act like you a saint just because Lamia is around. Do her like you do Rainey nigga," Ro rambled.

Tre gave him a death stare when he said that. Ro was just like a woman when he got mad. If he knew anything about you, it was bound to come out on mad day. At that moment, Tre was kicking himself for letting Ro in on so many personal aspects of his life. If any of his past misdeeds got back to Mia, she would run for the hills and never look back. He wasn't as innocent as he tried to make it seem during the two months that Mia had been holding out on him.

"We gon' see each other again," Tre promised Ro with a menacing stare.

"Make sure you tell Mia all of your secrets nigga. I would hate for her to find out from somebody else," Ro warned with a smirk.

"C'mon Tre," Mia said as she unlocked the doors and got in on the driver's side.

Duke made sure Tre got in before he left and went to his own car. Both men were his friends, but Tre was like the brother he never had. There was no question about where his loyalty was and would always remain.

"Are you okay?" Mia asked Tre as she drove off and got on the bridge.

"Yeah," he answered with a scowl.

Mia didn't want to press him, so she got off of the bridge at the first exit and headed towards her house. She could get Moonie's truck and go to the mall later. She wasn't trying to force Tre to be bothered if he didn't want to. She really wanted to ask him what secrets Ro were talking about, but she decided to leave the subject alone for now.

"Where are you going?" he asked.

"Home," Mia replied. "I'll get Moonie's truck and go to the mall later."

"Why? I told you that you could use the car. And I thought you were staying by me this weekend."

"I was, but you don't seem to be in the best mood right now. I just figured that you might want to be alone for a while. You don't seem like you want to be bothered."

160

"I just had a fight with one of my best friends Mia. I'm not in the best mood, but I always want to be bothered with you. You can pick Brandis up and just drop me off at home."

"Okay, but are we gonna talk about your secrets that Ro thinks you should tell me about?" She asked.

"I don't have any secrets Mia. You know how Ro is. He'll say anything to piss the next person off. Please don't fall for his bullshit. I have enough to deal with as it is. I really don't need us to be into it. I can't take that shit right now."

"I hear you, but if I find out some shit later on we're going to have a problem," Mia threatened.

"I know baby, but I'm good. I didn't do anything," Tre swore.

"Okay, just remember that I gave you a chance to tell me the truth," Mia replied.

She drove the rest of the way to Brandis' house in silence while Tre talked to Duke on the phone. Her gut told her that something was up, but she didn't have any proof. Tre never gave her a reason to think that he was doing anything wrong. Mia knew that she didn't have to go looking for anything. All she had to do was wait and everything would come to her in due time.

Chapter 12

By day three of their trip to Miami, Rainey was beyond ready to go home. They were having the time of their lives, but she was tired of feeling like the third wheel all the time. Mia and Brandis had Duke and Tre to chill with, but she was starting to feel like a pest. Even Von had Tanya to keep him company, but Rainey felt all alone. She talked on the phone with London or posted pictures on Facebook and Instagram all day. Then to make matters worse, she ended up bunking in the same room with Brandis and the man that she wanted for herself. It was supposed to be the women in one room and the men in the other, but that quickly changed. Their suites were connected by a door that allowed access to each other's rooms without going outside. Tre didn't think twice before he put Duke out of their room and moved Mia in. Thankfully, each room had two beds and a pullout sofa bed. Rainey and Brandis had their own beds, while Duke camped out on the sofa. It killed Rainey when the two of them would be all hugged up watching TV or sneaking kisses when they thought she wasn't looking. Not to mention when they had to hear Mia and Tre fucking like newlyweds all during the day and night. Von and Tanya were two floors up, so they didn't know what was going on.

"I wish her disgusting ass would have stayed home," Tre whispered to Mia.

"Who?" she asked just to be sure they were on the same page.

"I'm talking about Rainey. She's always frowned up like she doesn't want to be here anyway. She complains about everything that we want to do. This is your birthday trip and we're doing whatever you want to do. If she don't like it then she can stay in the room," Tre fussed.

They were walking in the mall and Rainey was lagging behind them talking on her cell phone. Duke and Brandis were in a shoe store while Tre followed Mia around trying to find her a sundress.

"What's up with you and her lately? Why does she make you sick all of a sudden?" Mia asked.

"That bitch woke up with an attitude for no reason. I swear this is her last time going anywhere with us with her hating ass. I don't even want you around her ass no more."

"It's not even that serious. She's probably salty because she sees Duke and Brandis together. You know she's had a crush on him since we were younger," Mia reasoned.

"But the man don't want her ass though. What part of that doesn't she understand? He made his choice and he didn't choose her. I wouldn't want her lil thin ass either if I was him. At least Brandis is slim with a lil shape. She's just straight up and down with no kind of curves and a pot belly," Tre frowned.

"Shut up Tre," Mia laughed.

Rainey wasn't as bad as he tried to make it seem. She was slender and had a very pretty face. Her caramel colored skin was flawless and her dark brown eyes had a slanted, exotic look to them. Although she had a head full of healthy hair, she still preferred her Brazilian weaves. Mia wouldn't call her stomach a pot belly, but it wasn't flat to say that she was so small. Brandis was slim too, but she had a shape with it. Her butt wasn't ridiculously huge, but she had more than a handful. Her dirty red complexion, bowlegs and sweet disposition was probably why Duke chose her over Rainey.

"I'm serious though, she's getting on my damn nerves with all that complaining."

Mia didn't know what the deal was between Tre and Rainey, but she didn't want to be put in the middle of it.

"Let's go in here," she said pointing to a store that had a bunch of sundresses on display in the window. Rainey sat down on a bench in front of the store while Mia and Tre went in.

"Try this one on," Tre said holding up a lime green tube dress for Mia to see.

"I like the dress, but not the color. I'm too dark for lime green. Find another color and I'll try it on," she replied.

She grabbed a few dresses that she liked and asked the clerk to let her into the dressing room. Tre came in a few minutes later with the dress he liked, in two different colors.

"Damn," Tre said when he saw Mia standing there in her pink lace briefs and matching bra. He tugged at the top of her underwear and she slapped his hand away.

"No Tre, we've been getting it in all day every day since we got here. You need to go sit out front if you can't keep your hands to yourself."

"Please Mia, five minutes," he begged.

"Wait Tre, I need to try these dresses on first."

"Okay, try the one I like on first then," he replied.

He replaced the lime green dress and got two more in red and a soft pink instead. Mia nodded and did what he asked her to. The dresses that Tre gave her was okay, but she thought the material looked cheap and made her butt look too big. He went crazy when he saw her in it and wanted her to get both colors. Five dresses later and Mia was ready to make her purchase and go. Aside from the two that Tre wanted her to get, she picked out three more dresses that she liked as well.

"No Mia, what the hell are you doing?" Tre roared when he saw Mia putting her clothes back on. He pulled her onto his lap and started kissing her neck.

"Wait until we get back to the room Tre. We have people with us and somebody is probably waiting to get into the dressing room," Mia whined.

"Man, that's all on them. You told me to wait until you tried on the dresses. Don't go back on your word now."

"I'm not," Mia smiled.

She grabbed his hand in hers and bought it up to her mouth. Tre's eyes bucked when she took his index finger and slipped it into her mouth and started sucking on it. She was looking directly into his eyes and he was in a trance. He couldn't look away even if he wanted to. When Mia released his finger, she grabbed his other hand and did the same thing with that one. Tre was going crazy and she seemed to enjoy toying with him.

"Stop playing with me Mia," Tre moaned as his entire body shuddered from the feel of Mia's mouth. She twirled her tongue around his fingers like a pro and he didn't want her to stop.

"I'm not playing. I want you to teach me how to do it," Mia whispered.

166

"Are you serious?"

"Yes, I'm very serious," Mia replied as she kneeled down in front of him.

Tre got excited when she started fumbling with the buckle of his belt. He'd received oral sex more times than he could count, but it was something special about Mia wanting to do it. Maybe it was because he knew that he was her first at something yet again. Once she had his pants undone, she just looked at him like she didn't know what to do next. Tre sprang into action and wasted no time pulling his rock hard erection out. Mia's eyes bulged and she wondered if she'd made a mistake. She remembered feeling like he was ripping her open when he took her virginity, now it seemed almost impossible to open her mouth wide enough for him to fit in. Her jaws ached just at the thought of it all.

"What's wrong Mia?" Tre asked when he saw the fear in her eyes.

"I don't know what to do. I'll choke to death if I put all of that in my mouth," Mia whispered making him fall out laughing.

"You don't have to put it all in your mouth. Just a little at a time, let me show you," he instructed.

Mia was nervous when Tre guided her head into his lap. She closed her eyes and opened her mouth a little waiting for him to shove himself inside. When nothing happened after a few seconds, Mia opened her eyes to find him staring at her with an amused smirk on his face.

"What?" she asked with an innocent shrug.

"How do you expect me to do anything with your mouth barely open? If it makes you feel better you can do everything on your own, just don't bite me," Tre joked.

"Okay, but you have to tell me what to do," Mia replied.

"I've never done it before so I don't know what to tell you," Tre smirked.

"Well, tell me what you like then smart ass," Mia replied.

This time she didn't close her eyes as she lowered her head once again and opened her mouth. Tre moaned in pleasure when he finally felt the warmness of Mia's mouth covering his pole. Instinctively, his hands went to the back of her head as it began to bob up and down.

"No teeth Mia," Tre whispered in between moans.

Mia was indeed a rookie, but that didn't stop her from making him feel damn good. He knew that with a little more time and practice, she had the potential be a pro. He wouldn't have a need for any outsiders once she got the hang of things. She would most definitely be the complete package then. Tre knew that people were probably waiting to get into the dressing room, but he threw his head back and allowed Mia to take him to paradise anyway. Nothing and no one mattered to him at the moment. Mia seemed to be getting into what she was doing, eliciting soft moans of pleasure from Tre. He wanted his moment of bliss to last forever. Unfortunately, it didn't last much than a few more seconds.

"Mia," they heard Rainey yell as she knocked on the fitting room door.

Mia pulled Tre's saliva drenched erection from her mouth and shot to her feet. She didn't miss the look of disgust and disappointment on his face due to their interruption. With a scowl on his handsome face, he stood up to fix his clothes while Mia made sure her appearance didn't reflect what they'd just done.

"Yeah Rainey," she finally answered.

"Are you okay in there? You've been gone for a minute," Rainey remarked.

Mia had been gone for almost thirty minutes and she knew it didn't take that long to try on dresses. She also didn't miss the fact Tre went into the room with her. Rainey just knew that she wasn't tripping. She clearly heard moaning coming from the room when she first walked up. That alone let her know that more than shopping was taking place behind the closed door.

"I'm good, I'll be out in a minute," Mia replied. Rainey walked away shaking her head in disgust. She regretted coming on this vacation with them, and they weren't helping her to feel any better.

"She's a fucking hater," Tre said angrily once they heard Rainey walk away. "I'm really starting to hate that bitch."

"First off, stop calling that girl a bitch," Mia scolded. "Don't even worry about it; we can always pick up where we left off."

"You promise?" he asked excitedly.

"Yes, I promise," Mia giggled.

"When?" Tre asked eagerly like it was his first time getting it done.

"Whenever you want to," she answered.

"I want to as soon as we get back to the room," Tre said making her laugh.

"C'mon, I need to go pay for this stuff," Mia said as she picked up the items that she wanted to purchase.

"I'll pay for it. I'm ready to go now," Tre answered.

He grabbed Mia's hand and almost dragged her to the cash registers. Once they were out of the store, they noticed Duke and Brandis had joined

Rainey on the bench. They had a few bags in their hands, but Rainey didn't buy anything.

"Where do y'all want to go next?" Brandis asked when Mia and Tre walked up to them.

"We're going back to the room," Tre hurriedly answered.

"What!" Mia yelled. "I'm not ready to go back yet."

"Yes you are," Tre said winking his eye at her. Not even five minutes later and she was going back on her word already. Mia grabbed him by his arm and pulled him away from everyone before she spoke.

"We are not going back to the room yet. You're starting to make me regret even going there with you. You said that we could do whatever I want to do and I want to finish shopping," Mia argued.

"Yeah alright, but don't forget what you promised me Mia."

"How can I? I just said it ten minutes ago."

"Okay, c'mon so you can finish spending all of my money. Don't try to break me. I still have to give you your birthday present when we get back home," Tre said.

"I told you that I have my own money. You don't have to spend yours. And why didn't you bring my gift here with you?" Mia asked.

"Maybe I couldn't," he winked as they walked away and joined their friends. "And I told you I want to give it to you on your actual birthday."

"So are y'all done shopping or what?" Rainey asked with a slight attitude.

She was starting to regret coming with them since they were taking so long. Mia was only supposed to be looking for a dress, but three hours later, they were still shopping. They probably would have been finished if she and Tre weren't doing God knows what in the fitting room.

"Rainey, you can go back to the room if you want to. It's only a few blocks away," Tre spoke up.

She looked over at him with hurt in her eyes at how he had been treating her lately. Ever since she tried to hook him up with London, amongst other things, Tre seemed to dislike her more and more. They used to get along just fine, but that hasn't been the case lately. She couldn't wait to get him by himself to see exactly what his problem was.

"I just asked a question Tank. All the attitude is not even necessary."

"I'm not the one with the attitude. You've been complaining since we got here. If you didn't want to come you should have stayed in New Orleans," Tre hissed.

"I'm not complaining. Even though Mia is calling all the shots, I still do whatever she wants us to do. I haven't done anything that I've wanted to do since we got here and we go home in two more days," Rainey responded.

"But you knew what it was before we came. It was Mia's idea for us to come here in the first place. I told everybody that it was her birthday trip and we were doing whatever she wanted to do. We've been talking about this shit for months. Don't try to act brand new because things aren't going your way," Tre yelled.

"We can do whatever you want to do Rainey. Nobody said anything, so I just assumed that y'all didn't care what we did. It's really not a big deal," Mia shrugged.

She refused to let Tre and Rainey's constant bickering, ruin her birthday vacation. They could argue when they got home, but Miami was off limits for drama.

"Fuck that Mia!" Tre yelled. "Nobody is going to ruin your birthday trip. I don't give a damn who it is."

"You're right and that goes for you too. I'm tired of all the back and forth arguing. We didn't come here for that. Let's just enjoy the rest of our time here and leave all the bullshit in the past. From now on, we'll all decide on what we're going to do. That way we'll be doing something that everybody agrees with," Mia said.

Tre wasn't feeling her little speech, but he decided to let it go for now. Rainey always wanted everything to be about her, but it wasn't happening on his watch. He didn't give a damn what she wanted to do. Mia was in charge and that was all there was to it. He looked over at Rainey and frowned, before he grabbed Mia's hand and walked off.

***

London was on the phone with Rainey listening to her talk about their not so fun trip to Miami that she'd just come from. They came back the night before, but it was too late for them to talk about it then. London had her on speakerphone since Cheryl was dying to know what happened. She was already in her feelings about Tanya being asked to go to Miami instead of her, but she insisted on hearing all of the details.

"So what happened after you and Tank's argument?" London asked.

"Nothing much happened after that. We really didn't say much to each other for the rest of the vacation. I mean, I understand that it was Mia's birthday trip and all, but that wasn't the reason for them giving her whatever she wanted. They always let her run shit and I'm sick of it. That was my last time going anywhere with them and I mean that," Rainey vented.

"I know I asked you this before, but I feel the need to ask again. Are you sure that Mia and Tank don't mess around? I can't see him doing so much for her just because she's his God sister. You're his God sister too, but he don't do nothing for you," London instigated.

"No they don't mess around," Rainey lied. She couldn't tell London the truth because that meant telling Cheryl too. If Von found out and they knew that she was the one who told on them, all hell would break loose. She hated keeping their secrets from them, but she really didn't have a choice.

"I still don't buy it. I think they mess around on the slick. She's a damn fool if she is messing with his ass. You and I both know that," London replied.

"They just feel like she has it so hard because of her mama and daddy, but that's bullshit. Mia has way more than me and her mama doesn't even have a job. Moonie don't mess with a man unless he has money and she knows how to get it out of all of them. To say she lives in the projects, Mia wears more Gucci and Chanel than all of us combined," Rainey informed them.

"What were Von and his bitch doing?" Cheryl asked.

"They weren't really with us too much. They did their own thing and we did ours. Their room wasn't even on the same floor as us," Rainey replied.

"Did she go back home or is she at Von's house?" Cheryl wanted to know.

"I'm the only one that went home. Everybody else went to Von's house. He and Tanya were talking about taking a trip to Vegas in a few months, just the two of them."

"I know you're lying," London yelled. She saw the somber look on her mother's face and instantly got upset.

"Nope, they said they needed to get away by themselves for a while. Von said that Tanya is always working and they don't spend enough time with each other. He's talking like he wants them to be together or something. She was another one who was catering to Mia the whole time. You know that's her Godmother right?" Rainey asked.

"Yeah I know, but that don't mean shit to me. I'll be damned if I sit back and let Von and Tanya be together after all the years I've put in with his ass. We'll be some old ass fighting heifers if they play with me," Cheryl said making Rainey and London double over with laughter.

"Did London show you the pictures that I posted online?" Rainey asked Cheryl.

"No, she didn't show me anything," Cheryl said while looking at her daughter.

"Tell her to show them to you. I'm going to bed. I'll talk to you tomorrow London," Rainey said before she hung up the phone.

"Why didn't you show me the pictures?" Cheryl asked her daughter.

"I wish Rainey wouldn't have said anything about that. You were already down about them being together and I didn't want to make it worse."

"I appreciate that London, but I'm a grown woman. I can handle anything that's thrown my way. Let me see the pictures," Cheryl requested.

London pulled up her Facebook account on her phone and logged in. She went to Rainey's page and pulled up her pictures before handing the phone to her mother. London watched in silence as Cheryl scrolled through the pictures and studied them one by one. She knew when she got to a picture of Von and Tanya because a frown instantly covered her face.

"Did you notice how Tank and Mia just so happened to be standing next to each other for every picture?" London asked her mother.

"Yeah I see. I'm starting to believe what you say. They do seem a little too close at times. Von must not be paying attention, but I'm about to help him open his eyes. Mia's not as innocent as they

177

think she is. Her mama ain't the only hoe in the family," Cheryl replied right before she got up and walked out of her daughter's room.

Chapter 13

"Happy birthday baby," Tre yelled into the phone once Mia finally answered for him. "What took you so long to answer?"

"Thanks Tre, but I was in the shower. You told me to be ready at ten. It's only a little after nine," Mia yawned. She wasn't used to getting up so early if she didn't have school, but Tre begged her to be ready. He was hyped about giving her whatever he got her for her birthday. She couldn't wait to see what it was because he was excited. The trip to Miami was good enough for her, but he insisted on giving her something else.

"Okay, get dressed and be outside at ten. I'll be down there waiting for you," Tre said before hanging up. Mia opened her walk in closet and began the hard task of finding something to wear for the day. She really didn't have anything planned, so she didn't buy anything new. Besides, she still had all of her new clothes that Tre got her in Miami. She had a million pairs of shoes, so finding a pair that matched wouldn't be a problem.

"Mia," Moonie yelled knocking on her bedroom door. Mia unlocked the door and opened it to let her in.

"You look cute. Where are you going?" Mia asked her mother.

She was dressed down in a pair of ripped jeans with a fitted shirt and a pair of cute wedges to match. Her hair was freshly done and she was pretty enough that makeup was never a part of her wardrobe. Moonie's shape was something serious even when she wasn't trying to show it.

"Thanks boo, I'm going somewhere with Dalvin. Happy birthday," Moonie smiled. She gave Mia a tight hug and handed her a gift bag that Mia never noticed before.

"The stuff in the bag is from me and Mitch and the card is from Dalvin."

"Thanks Moonie and tell Mitch and Dalvin thanks too," she said while sitting on her bed to see what she had.

She never had to worry about whatever her mother gave her because Moonie had great taste. She still shopped for Mia just as she did for the younger ones. Mia's face lit up when she pulled out a pair of Chanel sandals with the matching clutch. She also had two perfume gift sets and a few gift cards at the bottom of the bag. She then opened the card from Dalvin and pulled out the two hundred dollars bills that were stuffed inside.

"You like it?" Moonie asked although she already knew the answer.

"Of course I do. You know you always did shop for me better than I shop for myself," Mia said honestly.

"Do you have anything planned for today? I wanted us to go out to dinner. Just the two of us," Moonie said taking Mia by surprise. They hadn't done anything together by themselves since Mia was much younger.

"I'm going to take a ride with Tre in a few minutes, but I don't have anything else planned. Who's going to keep the kids?" Mia asked.

"They're going by Mitch's until tomorrow. You know that bitch Melissa is in her feelings. She always has a problem when the other kids come over, but she'll be all right. She better enjoy her time with my future husband while she can," Moonie said.

She was always saying that Mitch was going to be her husband one day, but she was too busy running the streets to make it happen. Mitch was always getting his kids to spend time with them, but he never left the other kids out. If Tootie and Desmond weren't with their father, he would get them and spend time with them as well. His girlfriend, Melissa hated when he got his own kids, but she really got pissed when he got the other two that didn't belong to him. Moonie had beaten her down more times than Mia could count, but she would still run off at the mouth every time they were around each other.

"Where do you want to go?" Mia asked.

"It's your day boo. We're going wherever you want to go. Just be ready to roll at seven," Moonie said before she exited Mia's bedroom.

Mia eventually decided on a pair of gray skinny jeans with a gray and purple crop top. She didn't know where they were going so she bypassed the heels and put on her purple, gray and white Air Max instead. It was right at ten when Mia finished curling her hair and spraying herself with perfume. She grabbed her purse and walked downstairs, right as Tre pulled up to the curb.

"You're timing is perfect. Where are we going?" Mia asked as soon as she got into the car.

"You could at least speak before you start asking questions," Tre said right before he pulled off. "Just sit back and enjoy the ride."

"Okay, but guess who invited me to dinner tonight?" Mia asked changing the subject.

"Who? I know you not playing with me with another nigga," Tre said looking at her like she was crazy.

"Why would I tell you if another man wanted to take me out? I'm not stupid. Moonie wants to take me out to dinner tonight. Crazy as it sounds I'm kind of excited about it," Mia admitted.

"It doesn't sound crazy at all. That's your mama. Despite y'all differences, you and Moonie are close," Tre replied. Mia was happy that they were on the subject of parents. She'd wanted to talk to him about a few things that were on her mind and now seemed liked the perfect time.

"If I really wanted you to do something, would you do it?" Mia asked.

"That's a stupid question Mia. I already do whatever you want me to do. All you have to do is ask and it's done," Tre assured her.

"Okay, well I want you to talk to Terri. It looks like she's really trying to do better Tre. I just keep thinking about how sad she looked when we saw her that last time. I know she messed up, but just give her a chance to explain herself. You never know, talking to her might make you feel better about the situation," Mia rambled trying to get her point across.

"I'm not making any promises Mia. I understand what you're saying and everything, but that situation is complicated."

"It's only as complicated as you make it. Will you at least think about it?"

"Yeah, I will," Tre said, hoping that she would just leave it alone.

"Okay, so are you going to tell me where we're going now?" Mia asked.

"You'll see where we're going when we get there," Tre said as he continued to drive.

He headed towards the Westbank Expressway and got on the bridge that took them into Jefferson Parish. They traveled in silence for about twenty more minutes until he pulled up into the parking lot of the Nissan dealership.

"What are we doing here?" Mia asked. She was hoping that he wasn't thinking about trading in his car because she loved his silver Challenger.

"A Nissan Murano right?" Tre asked her.

"What about it?" Mia asked.

"That's what you always said you wanted. Go pick out what color you like," Tre smiled at her.

"Stop playing!" Mia yelled as her eyes got twice their normal size. "You're getting me a fucking car for my birthday Tre?"

"If you don't want it we can leave and go get you something else," he joked. He knew that would never happen. Mia was infatuated with those trucks and she would die before she left without one.

"Ahhhh!" Mia screamed to the top of her lungs while kicking her legs in the air. "I can't believe you're getting me a car." She jumped on Tre's lap and started kissing him all over his face. He knew that she would be happy, but the way she was screaming made him laugh.

"C'mon, let's get out and look around," Tre told her. He didn't have to tell her twice. Mia jumped out of the car and was ready to go.

"Wait a minute Tre," Mia said as she thought about something. "What am I going to say when people ask who bought me a car? I don't work and you know Von is going to have a million questions."

"I don't know Mia. Tell them that Moonie got it for you."

"You know Von or Lamar are going to ask her about it. I'll get busted in a lie for sure if they do," Mia stressed.

"Well, say Jabari bought it for you," Tre replied.

"Jabari?" Mia yelled. "Why would Jabari buy me a car when he and Tiara are sharing one? And whose name is the car going to be in? I was hyped at first, but now I feel like I'm getting happy for nothing."

"You're eighteen now Mia, the car can go in your name. We'll figure out everything else later on. Don't start feeling down when you were just excited a minute ago. Let's go walk around," Tre said pulling her along with him.

A few hours later, Mia was all smiles as she drove off in her brand new sunset colored Nissan Murano Platinum. All of her fears were put to rest the moment she got behind the wheel. She was too excited for words to know that she would be driving herself to school for her senior year. Brandis was going to flip when she saw it. Of course the front seat would be reserved for her girl whenever she went somewhere. Their walking days were officially over and it felt damn good.

***

Two weeks later, Mia and Brandis were pulling up to the student parking lot at school. It was the first day, so they went early to eat the breakfast they bought and catch up with some of their friends. It was weird because they entered the building from a different way than they used to. The student parking lot was on the other side and they had to walk all the way around to get to where the other students were. As soon as they got out of the car, Rainey was pulling in right beside Mia's new truck.

"Who let you drive their car speed racer?" Rainey joked referring to how fast Mia drove.

"Check out the plates and you tell me," Mia replied. She had *Mz. Mia* personalized on her plates, so there was no mistaking that the car belonged to her.

"Oh shit, Von got you a car?" Rainey asked in shock. She felt a twinge of jealously, but she tried hard not to let it show. She had a car, but it was at the expense of her mother and stepfather. Von had absolutely nothing to do with it.

"What makes you think that Von got it for me? And whatever happened to you going to a private school? I thought Landry was too ghetto for you now," Mia inquired.

"I never said that," Rainey denied. "I just decided that I wanted to graduate with all of my friends instead of going somewhere where I don't know anybody."

Truth was her stepfather thought that it would be a waste of money to send her to a private school for her senior year. She didn't start out in private school and he didn't feel that she should end up there for her last year either.

"Did Tank buy this for you?" Rainey asked still trying to see who sponsored Mia's new ride.

"Why is that even important?" Mia asked.

"It's not, I was just asking," Rainey shrugged. They all walked towards the entrance and entered the front doors of the school together. As soon as they entered the school, they spotted Paige and her nieces arguing with one of the school counselor's in the hallway.

"They didn't even miss that many days last school year for y'all to fail them again. My nieces are going to be nineteen and twenty years old still in the eleventh grade," Paige yelled. Mia and Brandis walked right by them and laughed loud enough for them to hear. Rainey's friendly ass spoke to Paige as if they were the best of friends.

"What's funny bitch?" Shania yelled at Mia causing other students to stop and look their way.

"You see that Ms. Anderson?" the counselor asked Paige. "That's part of the problem. Your nieces can't seem to stay out of trouble. They've been suspended more than they've been in class. I told their father the same thing when he came to see me a few months ago. I can help them only if they're willing to help themselves. They don't even have enough credits to be classified as seniors."

"That's bullshit! My brother came and talked to you and you were supposed to help them get extra credit," Paige barked.

"You're absolutely right, but they never showed up to the credit recovery classes when they were supposed to. I'm sorry, but there is nothing that I can do. I'm going to tell you as I told their father. They might do better in a GED program because school does not seem to be working out for them," the counselor said before she turned and walked away.

By then Brandis and Mia were laughing uncontrollably, loud enough for everyone to hear.

Paige and her nieces wasted no time walking over to them, but one of the security guards stopped them before they got too far. He knew all too well about Mia and the sisters history. He lost count of how many fights he broke up between them the previous school year.

"We're good, I'm just coming to talk to my friend," Paige said pointing at Rainey. He nodded his head giving her the okay, but he stood close by just in case something popped off.

"What's up Paige?" Rainey asked her.

She knew that Paige and Mia had problems, but Rainey was always cool with her. She and Mia both used to hang out with her before Paige started suspecting Mia and Tank of messing around. Things went downhill for them after that, but Rainey didn't feel like she should have to choose sides in the matter.

"Nothing, but I'm trying to see what's so funny," she said looking over at Mia.

"The fact that your nieces are old enough to be teachers, but can't seem to get out of the eleventh grade is funny," Mia snickered as she winked at a male student who passed by and spoke to her.

"I see you got them hoe genes just like your mama. Both of y'all run around screwing everything in the hood," Paige replied.

"I can't speak for Moonie, but the only man that has ever been between my legs is…" Mia paused before she looked at Brandis and laughed.

"You can say it. I know you're talking about Tank. I don't know why y'all keep trying to hide it," Paige said getting upset.

"My God brother?" Mia asked as if she was appalled. "Why would you think I was sleeping with him? Just because I spend every weekend at his house and drive his car, doesn't mean that we're messing around. I'm kind of offended that you would say such a thing."

"I guess you feel like playing with me since you know security is going to stop me from beating your lil hot ass," Paige fumed.

"I'm not worried about you doing anything, but you should ashamed of yourself. You're too old to be coming to high school trying to fight the students," Mia taunted.

She knew that she was getting under Paige's skin by not giving her the reaction that she wanted. Paige lived for a good argument, but Mia refused to give her the satisfaction.

"It's all good. You know we'll see each other on the streets soon. If not, my girls always know where to find you," Paige said pointing to her nieces.

"Nah, you need to send somebody else at me. I'm tired of beating down the same people. Next time send somebody that can actually fight," Mia requested.

"Bitch you ain't ever beat none of us down," Shania yelled.

"Yeah okay," Mia brushed her off. "And what are you doing on this side of the building anyway? This area is for seniors only. Y'all are supposed to be on the other side with the juniors. I'm sure you know where it is since you've been a junior for the past five years."

"Let's go y'all," Paige instructed her nieces. "She gon' get hers. Her and her hoe ass mama."

"Bye Paige," Mia yelled after her. "I'll tell Tre and Dalvin that you said hello."

"You need to stop being so messy Mia," Rainey lectured once they were gone.

"You need to mind your business Rainey. I'm not the one who started it. She came to my school talking crazy to me. My heart pumps blood not Kool-Aid. I'm not scared of Paige and nobody else for that matter. She can get it right along with anybody else, including you," Mia threatened.

"Where did that come from? I don't have anything to do what's going on with y'all," Rainey said.

"You always say that, but then stand around and side with the next bitch. I don't know what's been up with you lately, but you better get your mind right when you come at me," Mia said right before she and Brandis walked away.

Rainey had been on some other shit lately and Mia wasn't feeling it. She hadn't really seen or talked to her since their trip to Miami and it was only for a few minutes if she did. She and London came to Von's house one night, but they left soon after discovering that Tanya was there. Mia hated what their relationship had come to, but that wasn't her fault. She wasn't about to kiss Rainey's ass just to be her friend. In her mind, Rainey was one less problem that she had to worry about.

Chapter 14

Rainey pulled up to Von's house and was happy that Mia wasn't there yet. She needed to talk to Tre alone. Their relationship seemed so strained lately and she needed to know why. Even Mia seemed to be distancing herself. They would speak to each other at school, but it wasn't the same as before. They barely talked when they were at Von's house and that made things somewhat awkward. Rainey knew that a lot of it was her fault and she wanted to make things right, starting with Tre.

"Hey Von," Rainey said when her Godfather opened the door for her. He was shirtless with a towel wrapped around his neck like he'd been working out.

"Hey baby," he said bending down to give her a kiss on the cheek. "I'm happy you came before I went back outside and finished cutting the grass. Tank is in his room, so you would have been knocking for a long time."

She wanted to tell him to give her a key like he gave Mia, but he never offered her one. Technically, he didn't offer it to Mia either, but he never asked for it back when she used it one time before. He gave it to her to let herself in when he wasn't home one time, but that had been over a year ago and she still had it. Von went back outside and Rainey put her clothes up in the bedroom where she always slept. As soon as she opened the door to go back into the living room, she spotted Tank walking down the hall.

"Hey," Rainey spoke.

"What's up?" he asked never bothering to look at her.

"Can I talk to you for a minute Tank?" Rainey asked while following him into the kitchen. He never answered, but he looked at her like he was giving her the okay to start talking.

"Say what you have to say Rainey," Tre snapped when she just stood there without opening her mouth. He pulled the cereal from the pantry closet and waited for her to say something.

"I'm really trying hard to see what I did to make you act like this towards me. You can't seem to stomach the sight of me and I don't know why," Rainey spoke up.

"Oh you don't?" Tre asked sarcastically.

"I've apologized to you a thousand times. I don't know what more you want me to say. I'm sorry for trying to hook you up with London and everything else that I did. I just hate the strain that my stupid mistakes have put on our relationship. We used to be so close now it's like you hate me. Even Mia is starting to act shady towards me," Rainey said on the verge of tears.

"She has every reason to act shady towards you, don't you think? You're not her friend and you never were. You're jealous of her and a blind man can see that. I wouldn't blame her if she never spoke to your hoe ass again," Tre ranted.

"So, I'm a hoe now Tank?" Rainey asked with tears in her eyes.

"If the shoe fits," he responded right as they heard keys opening the front door. A few seconds later, Mia and Brandis strolled in followed by Duke.

"Hey y'all," Mia spoke before opening the refrigerator and getting a bottle of water.

She joined the rest of them at the table, while Tre sat at the island eating a bowl of cereal. Brandis was showing them something on her phone, but Rainey wasn't paying attention. She got up and walked to the back room, slamming the door behind her.

"What's wrong with her?" Brandis frowned.

"I told y'all that she's been in her feelings for the past few weeks. At first I thought it was because of Duke and Brandis kicking it, but it seems like there's more to it than that," Mia shrugged.

The four of them talked for a while, until Von walked into the kitchen and started talking to everybody. Rainey must have felt better with him being there because she came out and rejoined them

195

not too long after. She had a somber look on her face, but nobody knew why.

"I don't know what y'all are going to do for food. Me and Tanya are going out to eat tonight," Von informed them.

Mia was looking forward to a hot meal, so she was more disappointed than everyone else. This was the only time she got one unless she cooked it herself. She was happy that her Godparents seemed to be getting closer, so she didn't mind ordering a pizza or grabbing some fast food.

"Where are y'all going out to eat at?" Duke asked.

"I don't know," Von shrugged right as the doorbell rang.

He walked away from his guests and opened the door in shock. He hadn't talked to Cheryl in a few days and he damn sure didn't invite her over. But there she was standing at his door with London's smiling face right behind her.

"Are you going to let us in or not?" Cheryl asked. Von was staring at her like she was a stranger, never once bothering to invite her in. Her feelings were hurt by the look of disappointment on his face.

"I was about to go somewhere, but y'all can come in for a little while," he said stepping aside.

Cheryl walked in and went straight to his bedroom, while London joined everyone else in the kitchen.

"Good evening everybody. Hey Tank," London spoke when she walked into the room.

"What's up?" Tre said never bothering to look up from his bowl of cereal.

Mia was cool with him speaking to them now and that was the only reason he opened his mouth at all. She still didn't like London or Cheryl, but she didn't want to put Von in a bad position. It was rude for Tre not to speak to his father's guests, so Mia let it go for his sake only. It would have been too weird if the same thing kept happening every time they came over.

"I didn't know that y'all were coming over here London," Rainey beamed. She was so happy to see her friend at the moment. At least she would have someone on her side for the time being.

"We weren't at first, but you know how my mama is. She was missing her man, so she decided to come over at the last minute. I didn't know that you were going to be here either until I saw your car parked out front. And when did you get a car Mia?" London asked. She was shocked when she saw the personalized plates on the new model SUV out front.

"Why?" Mia questioned with a frown. "I don't fuck with you and I'm not a pretender."

"I just asked. I didn't know your mama had it like that," London laughed to cover up her embarrassment at Mia's reply.

"Bitch, you don't know nothing about my mama. Mind your business before you get dealt with," Mia yelled standing to her feet.

London's breath was caught in her throat when Mia walked towards her. She was always throwing shade Mia's way, but obviously, she went too far this time. Tre stood to his feet and whispered in Mia's ear trying to calm her down. Mia was small in stature, but he could almost guarantee that London couldn't handle her in a fight. He saw her in action more times than he could count, and it was no match. London wasn't feeling the exchange between the two of them, but she knew better than to say anything.

"Calm down Mia, she was just joking," Rainey said coming to London's defense.

"I've been trying my best not to go there with you, but you already know you can get it too Rainey. We're not related by blood, so I don't have a problem fucking over you either," Mia warned. "Your stupid ass is always jumping in to rescue another bitch when you can't even help yourself."

When Rainey saw the heated look on Tre's face, she lowered her head and decided to shut up and stay out of it.

"What's going on?" Von asked when he re-entered the kitchen a few minutes later.

Mia looked like she was ready for war and Tre seemed to be acting as a mediator. Nobody said anything and he didn't bother asking again. He knew all of them well enough to know that they could keep a secret better than anyone else.

"Let's go London," Cheryl said when she came from the back of the house.

She looked like she'd been crying, but she kept her head down making it hard for anyone to really tell. London jumped up and almost ran to the door, and stood next to her mother like an obedient little girl. She was two seconds away from getting into her very first fight in all of her twenty years of living. She would rather die before she let Mia embarrass her in front of Tre.

"I'll call you later Rainey," London promised her friend right before they left.

"What's wrong Mimi?" Von asked Mia. She was the only one standing there with a frown on her face, so he asked her first.

"Nothing is wrong. I just had to put your stepdaughter in her place. I don't know why she's worrying about how I got my car," Mia answered.

"That's what she asked you?" Von wanted to know.

"Yep and that's why I went off on her."

199

"I see she's on that bullshit just like her mama," Von fussed.

"What happened with Cheryl?" Tre asked.

"She came at me about some shit that she saw on Facebook. I don't even do social media, so I don't know what the hell she's talking about. I never tried to hide the fact that Tanya came with me to Miami. She started all that crying and performing, so I told her ass that it was time to go. And why is London worried about what's going on with you Mimi? I'm still shocked that Jabari bought you a car too, but that's none of her damn business," Von fussed as he turned and headed back to his bedroom.

Mia and Tre locked eyes and smiled at each other, just like they always did. Rainey didn't miss the connection and that confirmed what she suspected all along. Tre had bought Mia a brand new truck.

***

"I need to talk to you about something," Tre told Mia as they lay in bed talking later on that night. Von had gone out with Tanya and everyone else was in the living room watching TV.

"What?" Mia asked as she turned her naked body around to face him.

Whenever he said he needed to talk to her she knew that it wasn't good. For his sake, he had better hope that he didn't say anything to piss her off. She made it known that if she left him again it was for good and she meant it.

"You remember when Ro was talking reckless when we had that fight not too long ago?" Tre asked.

"Yeah I remember. And do you remember me giving you a chance to come clean to me about anything that you were hiding that very same day? Your chances with me have run out Tre. If you're planning on telling me something that I won't like, you better prepare yourself for the single life. I'm nobody's fool and that includes you," Mia spat seriously.

"I know that baby, but listen to what I have to say before you talk about leaving me. You already know about it, but there's more to the story."

"I'm listening," Mia said giving him her undivided attention.

"You remember when I was by Paige when I was supposed to be by Duke's house? Well, you already know what went down with us, but Ro was there with me. When he was talking about me sharing you like I share the rest of them, he was talking about Paige," Tre confessed. Mia had a confused look on her face until she caught on to what he was trying to tell her.

"So, you and Ro had Paige at the same time?" Mia questioned.

"Yeah, but please don't get mad Mia. You asked me to be honest with you and that's what I'm doing. I wanted to tell you when you asked, but I was too mad at the time."

"What about Rainey? Did you have sex with her too?" Mia asked. She held her breath and waited for him to answer. She prayed that he didn't get down with Rainey because that was a deal breaker if he did.

"What?" Tre yelled. "No I didn't have sex with Rainey. I would never play you like that," he swore.

"Why did Ro say what he said then? He told you to do me like you do Rainey. What did he mean by that?" Mia wanted to know.

"He got down with Rainey a few times too. When he told me about it, I told him that I didn't give a fuck. He put all her business in the streets like she's a hoe, and she still went back for more. I guess he felt like he could get with you too since he got the green light to go after her. You already know that I wasn't having that shit. I don't give a damn about what Rainey does, but he went too far when he touched you."

"Both of y'all are trifling," Mia said speaking of him and Rainey. "She's running around here talking about everybody like she got her shit

202

together. Ro couldn't pay me to let his ugly ass fuck me on my worst day. And you sharing pussy with your friends like it's a blunt or some shit. Paige is too old and stupid to even let y'all play her like that."

"That shit was her idea. I was joking when I asked her to do it, but she made the shit happen for real. We talked about that a long time ago during one of my jail stays. I thought she forgot about it until she mentioned it to me again. I was talking about bringing another female in on it, but she's the one who got Ro involved," Tre replied.

"Nigga, you better not ever play with me like that. It don't even get that serious to keep a man."

"C'mon Mia, don't even go there with me. I don't want nobody to touch or even look at you for that matter. Why would I invite somebody else into the bed with us? I wasn't trying to go there with her ass, but that was all on her. She ain't my girl, so I don't give a damn," Tre shrugged.

"Is that why you and Rainey haven't been getting along lately?"

"Yep," he confirmed. "I tried to tell her stupid ass how Ro was throwing dirt on her name, but she wasn't trying to hear me. Then she went back and told the nigga everything that I told her. She was trying to make it seem like I was a hater when I was only trying to look out for her. I was done with her after that. I don't give a damn what them niggas say about her now. You don't know her like you think you do Mia. Rainey is an undercover hoe."

"Wow," Mia said shaking her head. She would have never thought Rainey would even give Ro the time of day. He was always flirting with everybody, but she was the only one dumb enough to fall for his weak ass lines.

"I need to tell you something else," Tre said causing Mia to sit straight up in the bed.

"Oh my God Tre!" Mia shrieked. "I can't take hearing nothing else. I'm going home."

When Mia tried to get out of the bed, he pulled her back and wrapped his arms tightly around her waist.

"It's nothing like that Mia. I just wanted to tell you that I talked to Terri," he hurriedly blurted out. She'd been on his back about calling his mama for weeks. He knew that she would be happy to know that he finally took her advice and made the call.

"Really?" Mia smiled and relaxed into his tight embrace.

"Yeah, we talked on the phone for a while. She wants me to go out to dinner with her soon."

"So, when are y'all going?" Mia asked excitedly.

"I don't know yet. I'm really trying to feel her out right now. It's like, she just woke up one morning and decided that she wants her kids in her life and I'm trying to find out why. What makes her want to be a mother now when we're all grown? Well, my brother and sister are still teenagers, but they're not babies anymore. I just feel like she has a motive behind everything that she does."

"There's only one way for you to find out," Mia shrugged.

Tre nodded his head and laid down with Mia resting comfortably on his chest. He was hoping that Von decided to stay the night with Tanya because he really didn't feel like getting up. It felt good when he could be with Mia without having to look over his shoulder or wonder if they were being watched. That was the only thing that he would change about their situation if he were ever given the chance. He wanted the world to know that they were together and he hoped that it would happen soon.

Chapter 15

Paige posted up on the bike that her new boo drove to the park and watched all of the activities around her. Her brother and nieces were a part of the social and pleasure club that came out to do their thing, along with several others. It was their annual Super Sunday celebration on the Westbank and the park where the second line ended was overly crowed as usual. To most Americans, "Super Sunday" is the Sunday on which the NFL Super Bowl is played. However, in New Orleans, Super Sunday has a different, totally unrelated meaning. It's a day for the city's Mardi Gras Indian tribes to put on their colorful suits, while marching in a procession through the streets of their neighborhoods.

Half-naked women pranced up and down the sidewalk, vying for the attention of anyone who offered it to them. The kids jumped in spacewalks, while most of the men showed off their bikes and newly washed cars. There were grills going all over the place, and Von was occupying one not too far from where she stood. He always had a tent set up for all of his friends and family, and today was no different. Moonie had a tent set up right next to his and Dalvin was right there with all of them. He didn't say two words to his own son, but he was out there throwing the football around with Moonie's kids as if he helped to create them. Paige's son didn't care because he was busy playing with his own friends, but she was pissed. Tre was also in attendance on his lime green and navy bike, but Mia was nowhere around. Paige saw him talking to a few females, but he passed her right up without uttering a word. Since she was with her new man, she decided to give him and her baby daddy a pass for the day. She didn't want to embarrass herself in front of everyone by causing a scene. She and Tre really didn't deal with each other anymore, but that didn't stop Paige from having feelings for her ex.

When he came to her house a few months ago and got all of his work, she knew that he was serious about being done with her. He told her that he didn't look at her the same after she was with him and Ro together, but she knew that was bullshit. He'd been acting distant with her long before that, but he used their threesome as his way out of her life. She regretted even acting upon one of his fantasies, but the damage was already done. It also didn't help that Ro was going around telling everybody about what happened between the three of them. Paige forgot about how much he talked, especially when it came down to somebody that was dumb enough to have sex with him. Of course, she denied it, but it was still embarrassing.

"I'm going take a walk and look for my brothers," Paige's new man, Dino said to her.

She kissed his lips and blushed when he lightly tapped her ass before walking away. Dino was only twenty-three years old, but he was much

207

more mature than Tre ever was when they were together. He actually wanted to settle down with her and he didn't care about her past. She sunk her hooks in him the same way she did Tre, and it seemed to have worked. He even spent time with her kids and that was something that Tre never did.

"You need to leave them young ass boys alone. And you wonder why you always out here fighting," Paige's brother, Peter said shaking his head.

He was the oldest out of the three of them and he was always fussing at her about one thing or the other. She and her brother, Shad were closer and he was never as judgmental as Peter. Shad didn't mind his daughters hanging out with Paige, but Peter kept his three kids far away from her if he wasn't around. He and his wife always looked down on her and Shad. Even thought they were out there celebrating the festivities with them that day, they hadn't seen them in months before that. Shad and her nieces lived in the same apartment complex as Paige, so she saw them just about every day.

"He's young, but he handles his business with me and my kids better than any man ever did. He takes care of them better than their own fathers. Dalvin is out here, but he hasn't said one word to his son. He's too busy playing daddy with the next bitch's kids," Paige snapped.

"I thought he said that Damon wasn't his?" Peter reminded her. "Did y'all take a blood test that I don't know about?"

208

"My son is his. He looks just like his no good dog ass," Paige fumed.

She was tired of Dalvin lying on her and denying their son. He begged Paige for a paternity test, but she refused. Her son was his, so there was no need for all of that. Damon was Dalvin's twin and everybody said so. He swore up and down that Paige's son wasn't his, but that never stopped him from coming around. He never really did much for Damon, but he stayed in Paige's bed more than she did. If he weren't with Moonie, he would still be coming around to get some. Paige knew that it was Moonie that stopped him from coming around altogether. She was really hurt because she and Dalvin were actually in a relationship at one time. The way he was acting made it seem like they had a fling and that simply wasn't true.

"Don't get mad with me. I'm just going by what he's been telling me and everybody else," Peter shrugged in and uncaring manner.

He had a smirk on his face letting Paige know that he was enjoying his insults just a little too much. Arguing with him would only turn out bad, so she closed her mouth and let the conversation end with him having the last word. Paige posted up with her nieces and watched the action, trying hard not to let her brother's words ruin her day. As much as she tried not to, her eyes kept wandering over to where Tre was. He looked so good in a simple white tee and blue jeans. He rode up and down the park with his friends like he didn't have a care in the world. He passed by Paige and her family several times, but he never even looked her way. Knowing the history that they once shared, that hurt even more than Dalvin's denial of her son.

"Paige look," her niece Shania, said pulling her away from her thoughts.

Paige looked up right as Mia and Brandis exited a cute colored SUV. Her voice was caught in her throat when she saw the personalized plates that adorned the rear of the truck. There was no doubt in her mind that the vehicle belonged to Mia, but her mind was swimming with thoughts of who purchased it for her. Her first thought was Von, but she didn't rule Tre out either. Then the possibility of Moonie getting the money from Dalvin to buy it wasn't impossible, seeing as how she had him wrapped around her finger.

"I wonder how many dicks she has to suck every month to pay the note on that," Paige joked making her nieces laugh.

"Girl, check them out," Shania instigated, as they all watched Mia and Brandis hop on the back of Duke and Tre's bikes. "They can lie all they want to, but something is going on with them."

"I already know," Paige agreed. And just like always, Peter had to put his two cents in.

"So you're out here with another man, but you're still worrying about Tank?" he asked shaking his baldhead in disgust. "So what if he is messing with her? At least she's in his age group."

That last comment did it for Paige. She was sick of her brother's mouth and was ready for him and his entire family to go home.

"Just in case you forgot I'm a grown ass woman. If you don't like what I do or how I do it stay the fuck from around me. You always have something to say, as if your family is perfect. I like it better when you stay away," Paige snapped right before she walked off with her nieces in tow.

"I'm so happy you told his ass off," Shania said as she followed behind her auntie.

Her uncle Peter was always making her and her sister feel bad about one thing or another. He put his daughters and son on a pedestal, but they weren't as perfect as he thought they were. His oldest daughter was a slut and the youngest one was following right in her footsteps.

"He needs to get his ugly ass wife and his ugly ass children, and go home. I'm tired of him always minding my business," Paige fumed.

"He does the same thing to our daddy. He's always telling him that he's raising us wrong. His kids are no better, but he can't see that," Sariah chimed in.

The three of them continued to talk about Peter as they made their way over to a group of people dancing near the DJ. Paige kept her eyes trained on Tre while he zipped up and down the street with Mia seated on the back of his bike. She had her arms wrapped tightly around his waist with a huge smile adoring her face. Paige wished she could snatch her off the next time they passed by, but that wasn't possible without a few people trying to kill her. Mia and Moonie were two people that she wished she could get rid of permanently.

***

"Mia, go straight home and I'm serious," Tre said as he walked Mia to her truck. "You know anything is bound to pop off around here after a certain time."

The Super Sunday festivities were coming to an end, but that didn't mean that everyone would go home. Most times people hung around the park just to see if a fight or some other kind of action would take place. A few times, shots had rung out causing people to panic and trample each other, trying to get away. Tre didn't want Mia around if anything happened and he was happy that she decided to go home early. Brandis had already left with Duke, so she would be riding home by herself.

"I am going straight home Tre. I have school tomorrow," Mia replied.

"Okay, call me once you get settled. I love you." He wanted to kiss her, but he knew that she wasn't having it, especially with Von being so close by.

"I love you too," Mia answered before getting in her car and pulling off.

As soon as she turned the corner, she went in the opposite direction from her house. She needed gas and she didn't want to leave for school earlier than usual to get it. The gas station was two minutes away from the park and that was perfect. Mia pulled into the almost empty station and pulled her debit card out to pay. Once she had the gas pump going, she used that as an opportunity to throw away some empty water bottles from her cup holders that she and Brandis left there earlier. About three minutes later, Mia heard the clicking of the gas pump letting her know that her car was full. When she pulled the pump out, she looked up just in time to see Paige and Shania walking towards her. Since Mia wasn't scared, she took her time replacing the pump and securing her gas cap.

"So what was all that hot shit you were talking at your school a few weeks ago?" Paige asked her.

"You mean the part about you being too old to be fighting high school students or the part about your nieces being too old to be high school students? I said a lot of hot shit that day, so you have to remind me," Mia flippantly replied.

"You're real cute," Paige chuckled sarcastically.

"Thank you," Mia replied. "Everybody says that, especially Tre."

"Real funny bitch... Shania hit that hoe," Paige ordered her flunky of a niece.

Before Shania had a chance to react, Mia was hitting her first. Paige was yelling, trying to coach her niece on what to do next, but it wasn't helping much. Mia was shorter than her, but she was clearly winning the fight. Paige tried to pull them apart, but Mia's hold on Shania was too strong.

"Get off of me," Mia yelled when she felt Paige pulling her shirt.

She held Shania with one hand while shoving Paige away with the other. It took everything in Paige not to hit her much younger opponent. Instead, she yelled for Sariah to come over and do it for her.

"Don't just stand there and let her get the best of your sister. You better come over here and handle your business," Paige demanded.

Mia didn't know if Sariah had come over or not until she felt her hair being pulled from behind, followed by a series of licks. She tried to keep all of her focus on Shania, but it was becoming too hard. In a matter of seconds, she turned around and unleashed her fury on the other sister. Mia was outnumbered, so once again she was being pulled in two different directions. She was getting tired, but she refused to give up. She felt them trying to pull her to the ground, but she wasn't going down that easily. They would probably stomp her like a dog if she did.

"Hey, break that shit up," a male voice yelled in the distance.

The sisters kept right on swinging, so Mia did the same. She was already being jumped and she didn't want to make it worse by not defending herself. A few seconds passed before Mia felt someone pulling them apart. Whoever it was grabbed Sariah first, so she used that as an opportunity to really focus on the sister. She grabbed Shania's hair and rained a series of blows to her face.

"Don't just grab my nieces and let that bitch get the best of them," Paige yelled.

"You better get your nieces and get the hell out of here before all of y'all be going to jail," he warned. "You're wrong for standing by while they jumped that damn girl anyway."

Mia was still swinging like crazy until he felt herself being lifted from the ground.

"Let me go," she yelled, kicked and screamed.

"Calm down lil mama. Come inside and call somebody to pick you up," the unknown man requested.

Mia didn't immediately look in his face, but she did see that he was an employee of the gas

215

station just by the uniform shirt that he wore. She calmed down a little when he opened the door and placed her feet on the floor. She looked out of the window and saw Paige and her crew piling up into her barely working Toyota Camry. They peeled out of the parking lot, leaving a trail of smoke behind them.

"Should we call the police?" the female cashier asked the other employee.

"Nah, I think they're gone. You have a phone to call somebody to pick you up?" he asked Mia.

"Yeah, but my phone is in my car," she replied.

"I can go get it for you or you can use the store's phone," he offered.

"Yeah, here you go, just use this one," the cashier suggested handing her the cordless phone. She grabbed a stack of paper towels and handed them to Mia. "You're lip is bleeding."

"Thanks," Mia smiled weakly. "Is there a bathroom that I can use?"

The cashier pointed the way and Mia walked off, while dialing Tre's phone number at the same time. She knew that he was going to be pissed, especially because he asked her to go straight home and she didn't listen.

"Yeah," Tre yelled into the phone. Mia was happy that he answered because he usually didn't if the number was unknown to him.

"Where are you Tre?" Mia asked him.

She examined her face in the mirror waiting for him to answer. Aside from a few scratches, busted lip and her wild hair, Mia didn't look like she'd been in a fight with not one, but two people at the same time. The sisters couldn't really fight one on one and apparently they couldn't fight together either. Since they wanted to jump, Mia knew that it was far from over between the three of them.

"Mia?" Tre asked like he was unsure.

"Yeah, where are you?" she asked again.

"I'm still at the park. Why are you calling me from another phone? Where are you?"

"I'm at the gas station around the corner from the park. That bitch Paige got her nieces to jump me."

"What!" Tre yelled angrily. "Stay right there, I'm on my way."

Mia hung up the phone and wet the paper towels in her hand. After cleaning the blood from her lip, she fixed her hair and splashed cold water on her face before going back to the front of the store.

"Thank you, my God brother is on his way," she said handing the phone back to the cashier.

"You're welcome baby, just stay in here until he pulls up," the older woman suggested.

Mia nodded and stood near the counter and peered out of the window. The guy that helped her was out front sweeping, but Mia wanted to thank him too.

"There he is, thanks again," Mia said when she saw Tre pull up on his bike.

She walked out front and thanked the man who helped her, before walking over to her car to talk to Tre. She saw the frown on his face before she even made it over to him.

"What the fuck happened, Mia?" he yelled while grabbing her face to inspect it.

"I already told you what happened. Those scary bitches jumped me."

"Why don't you listen, Mia? I told you to go straight home and that's what you should have done. All of this shit could have been avoided," he fussed.

"Stop talking to me like I'm your child. I needed gas, so I came to get some. It's not my fault that your bitch can't let go," Mia snapped.

"I'm so done playing games with Paige and her nieces. Get in your car and let me follow you home," he instructed.

Without uttering another word, Mia hopped in her car and headed towards her house, with Tre following close behind on his bike.

***

The next day, Tre was outside of Mia's school twenty minutes before the bell rang at the end of the day. He tried convincing her to stay home, but she refused. She'd only been back in school for a few weeks and she didn't want to start missing days already. She made it clear that she wasn't scared and he had no doubt in his mind about that. Besides, the seniors were located in an area of the school of their own. They didn't have to fraternize with the other grades, or even see them for that matter. Since he wasn't there to see Mia, he waited on the side that the ninth through eleventh graders entered and exited. As soon as the bell sounded, Tre watched the students file out of the building until he spotted who he was looking for.

"What's up y'all?" he spoke when he saw Paige's nieces walk out.

"Hey Tank," Shania said smiling hard.

Out of the two sisters, Tre disliked her the most. She was messy and she was always reporting to Paige about everything that went on. Sariah was more of a follower and did everything that her sister told her to do. She was the quiet one, but she came out of her shell just to please other people.

"Let me talk to you for a minute Shania," Tre said stopping her in her tracks.

He was leaned up against his bike, so she walked over to where he stood. He was actually talking to both of them, but Shania was always the mouthpiece for her sister anyway.

"Okay, what's up?" she questioned.

"I don't know what Paige has been telling y'all, but we are not together and we haven't been together for a while. Mia don't have shit to do with whatever is going on with us and neither do y'all. For y'all to jump her last night was going too damn far," Tre spat angrily.

"Nobody jumped her scary ass," Shania lied. "She got her ass whipped and now she wants to claim that she got jumped."

"So you and this simple looking bitch didn't jump her when she was at the gas station last night?" Tre asked while pointing to Sariah.

"My sister ain't simple. Like I just said, I whipped her ass and I did it by myself. If she has a problem with it, she can come see me for round two," Shania countered.

"You got that, round two it is," Tre smirked right before he got on his bike and pulled off.

"Fuck him," Shania spat angrily. "I can't wait to tell Paige about his stupid ass. Let's get to this bus stop before we miss our bus."

Just like always, Sariah followed behind her sister with no questions asked. She really wished her sister and aunt would just leave the situation with Tre alone, but they weren't letting up. Thanks to them, she would probably die before she made it out of the eleventh grade. Her grades weren't all that great, but they were good enough for her to pass had she not missed so many days from being suspended all the time. They were cool with Mia at one time, but she was definitely the enemy now. Every time Tank did something to make Paige mad, she took her frustrations out on Mia. If it weren't for her pushing them up to fight her, they probably never would have done it. For the first time in a long time, Sariah decided to speak up about how she felt.

"I'm getting tired of all this drama behind Paige and Tank. If he doesn't want her, she needs to move on and let that shit go. She already got another man anyway. Next time she wants somebody to fight Mia, she better do it herself," Sariah said surprising her sister.

Sariah usually went with the flow of things, but she must have really been fed up to speak on it. Paige had been like a mother to them since their mother died some years ago. Aside from their grandmother, she was the only other female who they could depend on. Their mother was stabbed in a fight when they were only ten and eleven years old, and they'd been with their father ever since. He basically didn't care what they did and Paige had them doing all kinds of shit.

"I'm starting to feel the same way," Shania said agreeing with her sister, as they walked up to their bus stop. They still had a few more minutes to wait, but she was happy that they didn't miss it.

"Here comes Tank stupid ass again," Sariah said when she saw him pulling up on his bike.

"So about that second round," Tre said directing his comment more towards Shania.

She was tired of going back and forth with him, but he needed to know that she wasn't scared of him or Lamia.

"Tell Mia whenever she's ready, she knows exactly where to find me," Shania replied.

"Who said that your second round was going to be with Mia?" he asked with a smirk.

"Are you going to fight me for her?" Shania said as she and her sister laughed.

"Nah, I don't fight girls, even if they do look like men," he laughed. "But I got somebody who's willing to go a few rounds with you."

He whistled and a group of four girls that the girls never even noticed before, hopped out of a black Tahoe. No words were said, as they raced over to the sisters and commenced to beating them down right at the bus stop. The first hit that Shania felt was almost like a brick being thrown in her face. The ones that followed were no better. Her face was on fire and her ears were ringing. There was no way that she and Sariah were winning the fight, but she swung back anyway. Shania prayed that her sister was making out better than her, because she was getting her ass kicked up and down the sidewalk. She knew that a crowd had formed just by all the yelling and other noises that she heard around them. People were actually cheering the fight on instead of trying to break it up.

"Stomp that hoe," somebody in the crowd yelled causing Shania to panic. Her sister must have fallen and someone was encouraging her attackers to finish her off.

"Get them off of me," Shania yelled hoping that someone came to her rescue soon.

She was growing weaker by the second and she now knew how Mia felt when they did the same thing to her the night before. They had only been fighting for a few minutes, but the pain made it feel like hours.

"I thought you wanted round two," Tre taunted Shania, while she continued to get the beat down of her life. He must have paid those girls a grip to fight them and they were putting in overtime. The sisters had just decided that they were done fighting with Mia, but it was too late. They took it too far when they jumped her and Tank wasn't having it. If she could take it back to avoid the situation they were in right now, she would. She was sure that Sariah was probably feeling the same way.

"Hey y'all, I think somebody called the police," a man yelled from the crowd. That was music to Shania's ears. She needed something or someone to bring her nightmare to an end and the police was perfect.

"Let's move around y'all. I think they got the point," Tre said.

Just as fast as the fight started, it stopped and Tre and his female accomplices were gone in a matter of seconds. The crowd of people started to disperse, but not before some of their classmates laughed and let the girls know that the entire fight had been recorded. As if things weren't already bad enough, they now had to worry about the entire school as well as everyone on social media hearing about it or seeing it. They would have to relive their nightmare for a long time.

"Ahhh," Shania cried out in pain when she tried to lift herself up on one hand.

"Look at your hand and wrist," Sariah yelled excitedly. Shania's hand was throbbing like crazy, but it, along with her wrist, had started to swell as well. It almost looked like it was deformed or crooked.

"It hurts too badly for me to even use it to get up. Call daddy or Paige to come and pick us up," she ordered her sister.

They knew without a doubt that Tre was going to see their father, whether he wanted to or not. Shad didn't play about his only two daughters and Tre was going to find that out the hard way.

Chapter 16

Tre sat in front of the restaurant and gathered his thoughts before going inside. He looked down at his ringing phone and declined another one of Paige's calls. She'd been blowing his phone up for three days straight and he didn't answer for her one time. She'd even left a few messages cursing him out for having her nieces jumped. When they jumped Mia at the gas station after Super Sunday, all of Tre's common sense went out of the window. He called his cousin Tae and some of her friends, and it was over from there. Tae parked her Tahoe right at their bus stop and waited for Tre to give her the green light to put in work. He knew that they couldn't fight them on school grounds without going to jail, so their bus stop was the perfect place. The look on the sisters' faces when Tae and her crew came at them was priceless. He didn't care about how Paige or anyone else felt when it came down to Mia. He warned her about what would happen, but they must have been taking him for a joke. Mia could handle herself in a one-on-one fight, but they took it to another level when they jumped her. The joke was on them this time because they had been fucked all the way up. When the phone rang again, he was about to decline, but he decided to answer it this time.

"What the fuck you keep calling my phone for Paige?" he yelled angrily.

"You know why I'm calling your phone, so don't play dumb nigga. My fucking nieces are walking around here with a broken hand and black eye thanks to you getting them jumped. They have to go to a GED program because they can't even go back to school," Paige screamed.

Shania's wrist and hand were broken as a result of trying to block some of the licks to her face. In addition to having a patch of her hair pulled out, Sariah also had a black swollen eye to go along with it. They were too embarrassed to go back to school in their condition, so Paige and their father removed them from the school's enrollment. When they were completely healed, they would have to register to get a GED instead.

"I don't give a fuck about none of that. Those bitches are too old to still be in high school anyway. They should damn near be in their senior year of college. I already told you what it was the last time they got into it with Mia. They need to stay in their fucking lane and you need to do the same."

"All that behind a bitch that you ain't fucking? It's all good though. You know my brother don't play behind his girls. You gon' see him real soon. You can bank on that shit," Paige threatened.

"You think I give a damn about seeing your brother? Fuck you, him and his daughters, straight like that," Tre said before he hung up in her face.

He didn't know the severity of Paige's, nieces' injuries, but he really didn't care once he was informed. He wanted Shad to come at him wrong and he would lay his ass out too. It wouldn't be the first time something popped off between the two of them. He tried checking Tre behind Paige once before and got his ass beat.

"Fuck them," Tre mumbled to himself while getting out of the car.

He'd wasted enough time sitting in his car and he was ready to get the conversation that he was about to have over and done with. When he walked into the restaurant, he spotted who he was looking for sitting at a table in the rear of the dining area. Tre made his way over and took a seat at the only empty chair.

"Hey baby, I'm so happy that you decided to come," she smiled brightly.

"What's up Terri?" Tre asked greeting his mother.

She'd been asking him to meet her for a while and thanks to Mia, he finally decided to come. They were long overdue for a talk, but he wasn't sure that he was ready to hear what she had to say. He tried to act like her not being a part of his life was no big deal, but the truth was that it hurt him more than he cared to admit. Mia knew how he felt, but he never expressed his feelings to anyone else, not even Von.

"Not much, I just wanted to catch up with you. You know, see how you're doing and what's new in your life," Terri beamed.

"You can't be serious," Tre frowned. "I'm twenty-one years old and you're just now trying to see what's going on with me? I've been in and out of jail most of my life and you never even sent a letter, but you want me to believe that you're concerned about me all of a sudden?"

"I know what you're thinking, but it's never too late for anything. As long as we have breath in our bodies, there's always hope."

"I hate to burst your bubble, but it's been too late for us. You pretty much said fuck me the day you gave me and all of my belongings away to Von. Thanks for the invite, but I'm not interested in fixing a relationship that never existed in the first place," Tre said standing to his feet. He was about to walk off, but Terri's next words stopped him in his tracks.

"I'm dying Tank," she blurted out quickly.

"What?" he asked just to be sure he heard her correctly.

"I'm dying," she repeated. "I have full-blown aids."

Hearing her say that damn near knocked all of the wind out of Tre, causing him to take his seat once again.

"I was given an HIV diagnosis a few years ago, but I just found out that it's turned into full-blown aids as a result of me not taking care of myself the way that I should have," Terri continued.

"How?" he mumbled.

"Honestly, I'm really not sure. I'm embarrassed to say it, but I've been with so many men that it's almost impossible for me to know who gave it to me. I don't even know if I've passed it along to someone else. I would have never known if I hadn't gone to the hospital one night. I had a fever for three days straight and they did some blood work on me. I found out a few days after that, but I was in denial. I kept living my life as if nothing was wrong. It wasn't until I got this last doctor's report a year ago that I knew it was really serious."

"Damn. So, there's nothing that they can do for you? What about medicine or something?"

"I had medicine that I should have been taking when I was diagnosed with HIV to help increase my T-cells. I didn't take it and my cell count dropped too low, which is how I was diagnosed with the aids virus. I've just learned to accept my fate. I'm going to die," Terri replied.

"Stop saying that. You just said there's always hope as long as you have breath in your body. Don't give up on your life like that."

"I've made peace with God and now I want to do the same with my family. I also wanted to talk to you about some important information."

"Okay."

"I want you to handle all of my final arrangements. I know that this is a lot to ask, but I really need you to do this for me. I have two insurance policies. One for you and the other is for your brother and sister. When I die, you'll have a nice lump sum to live off of for a long time. Your policy is the biggest since you're my firstborn," she smiled.

"I don't want to benefit off of your death Terri. You know I'm good on money, and I really don't know if I'm the right person to do what you're asking. I don't know the first thing about planning a funeral."

"I already have everything written up just the way I want it. All you'll be doing is following my instructions. I'll be buried in my family's plot and I want my services to be in the church that I grew up in. I really need you Tank. Your brother and sister basically said that me being sick is God's way of punishing me, and their father agrees. He's pretty much turned them against me, not that I blame him. His wife has been more of a mother to them than I've ever been. They've basically said that they don't want anything to do with me. At least they'll both be fifty thousand dollars richer when I die. The policy that's in your name is two hundred fifty thousand. Once you bury me, the rest is yours."

Tre didn't know what to say. He really didn't know Terri like a child should know their mother, but his heart still hurt for her. He was about to say something else until the ringing of his phone stopped him.

"I'll have to call you right back Mia, I'm still talking to Terri," he said answering his phone. He listened to Mia's reply before disconnecting his call and giving Terri his undivided attention once again.

"So, does Von know about you and Mia?" Terri smirked.

"What do you mean does he know about us? What's there to know?"

"C'mon now Tank. I might not have raised you, but I still have my maternal instincts. How long have you and Lamia been sneaking around?"

"A little over a year," he confessed. "Please don't mention this conversation to nobody Terri. She would kill me if she knew that I was talking to you about it. She's scared to death of Von finding out."

"My lips are sealed. I understand how she feels though. Von loves Mia like his very own, so he probably won't understand y'all being together. I hate that y'all have to sneak around because I can tell that you really have feelings for her."

"That's my baby, but I kind of understand her feelings too. It just gets frustrating that we can't be together out in the open like I want us to," Tre shrugged.

"It'll get better," Terri said while grabbing his hand.

"I hope things get better for you too," he replied squeezing her hand.

***

"I guess Von started kicking it with this bitch again," Mia frowned when she saw Cheryl's car parked in Von's driveway.

He and Tanya had been hanging a lot lately, but it looked like Cheryl had finally made her way back in. It was nice not having to see her and London every weekend, but that was all over with now.

"You know she wasn't giving up until Von came around," Brandis replied.

She and Mia walked into the house, and were surprised to find Rainey and London sitting on the sofa, talking like old friends. Rainey spoke when they came in, but London turned her head without uttering a word. That was fine with them because Mia and Brandis didn't want to speak to her anyway.

"Where's Von?" Mia asked.

"He's in his room with Cheryl," Rainey answered.

"Von," Mia yelled calling her Godfather into the living room.

"That's so rude, he's obviously busy," London rolled her eyes.

"Brandis, get this bitch a Band-Aid. It must really hurt for her to mind her own business. I'm sure Cheryl taught you how to speak only when you're being spoken to," Mia snapped.

"She just told you that Von was in the room with his girlfriend and you're calling him anyway," London went on.

"His girlfriend?" Mia shrieked. "I hope you and your mama are not dumb enough to think that. Von is a ladies man and Cheryl ain't his only lady."

"Like father like son," London laughed, even though Mia didn't get the joke. Rainey and Brandis remained quiet while the two of them continued to go back and forth.

"Pick your battles London. This is one that you don't want. Cheryl might not spank that ass anymore, but I really don't mind," Mia threated right, as Von came out of the room with Cheryl following close behind him.

"What's up Mimi?" he asked.

"Lamar said to tell you that he's waiting on you. He said that y'all are supposed to be going somewhere," Mia replied.

"Yeah, I'm going to get him in a few minutes. I tried calling him earlier, but he didn't answer."

"His phone is acting crazy. That's why he asked me to tell you," Mia replied.

"Where are we going?" Cheryl asked.

She was standing behind Von holding on to his arm like she was afraid that he was going to run away. Mia wanted to throw up when she said "we" like she and Von were a packaged deal.

"I need to make a run right quick. You can stay here or I'll call you when I come back," Von replied.

"You know I'm not going anywhere," she giggled like a schoolgirl as she walked back to the bedroom. London looked at Mia and smirked as if to say, "I told you so." Mia was done entertaining her for the day. She really felt like slapping her in the mouth, but she decided to let her make it for now.

"Hey Tank," London cooed when Tre walked into the house carrying a huge brown envelope. She was smiling hard making her almond shaped eyes practically disappear.

"What's up," Tre spoke to everyone.

He briefly made eye contact with Mia before going straight down the hall to his bedroom, closing the door behind him. Mia knew that something was wrong and that was her reason for being there on a school night. Tre sent her a text telling her that they needed to talk and she rushed right over. She knew that it had something to do with Terri, because he'd met her for lunch earlier that day. She wasn't worried about London and Cheryl, but she couldn't go to his room with Von still being home. He was getting ready to leave, so she sent Tre a text letting him know that she would be there as soon as he did. About ten minutes later, Von came from the back of the house fully dressed and ready to go.

"I'm leaving too, I have homework," Rainey announced as she stood to her feet and walked to the door. As soon as Mia heard them pull off, she got up too.

"I'll be right back Brandis," Mia announced to her friend. She headed straight down the hall to Tre's room and lightly tapped on his door. London wanted to get up and see where she was going, but she didn't want Brandis to tell Mia that she was spying on her.

"Did Von leave?" Tre asked her when he opened the door for her.

"I wouldn't be in here if he didn't," Mia replied. "How did it go with Terri?"

"I feel like shit Mia," Tre said as he pulled her down and sat her on his lap.

"Why, what happened?"

"All these years I've been walking around here hating her for abandoning me, and now she's dying."

What? How is she dying?" Mia inquired.

"She has aids."

"Damn Tre, I'm sorry to hear that," Mia said while rubbing his back.

"But that's not the worst part of it. She wants me to handle all of her funeral arrangements when the time comes. Look at this," he said lifting her off of his lap and handing her the brown envelope that he walked in with.

Mia opened it and her mouth dropped to the floor. Terri had everything planned out for her funeral with every little detail in place. She wrote down what she wanted to wear on down to what kind of flowers she wanted next to her casket. When Mia got to the insurance policy, she was really in shock. Terri made Tre the beneficiary on a quarter of a million dollars. She would be doing more for him in death than she ever could if she were alive.

"How do you feel about all of this?" Mia asked him.

"I really don't know how to feel. It's like I wanted to tell her that I couldn't do it, but I didn't have the heart. You know I'm really going to need your help when the time comes Mia. I know Von will help me, but I need you too."

"You know I'll help you any way I can," Mia promised.

"I appreciate you baby. Oh, and Terri asked me how long have we been messing around," Tre laughed.

"You told her?" Mia yelled.

"No, she asked me if Von knew about us. I tried to play it off, but she wasn't hearing it. She must have figured it out on her own. Damn near everybody knows what's going on except for Von. We might as well tell him and make this shit official. He probably thinks I'm gay since I never bring any females over here. I'm tired of feeling like I'm single when I have a girl. We have to sneak and spend time together like we're kids and shit," Tre fussed.

"How did we go from talking about Terri to you talking about us?" Mia questioned.

"Because this shit is getting old Mia. I'm trying to be patient, but I'm tired of doing this. You know I got you no matter what happens. Von is with who he wants to be with and we should be able to do the same."

"Okay Tre," Mia mumbled while fidgeting with her fingers.

"What does okay mean Mia?"

"We can tell him, but let me tell you when I'm ready."

"That's a deal breaker right there. You haven't been ready in over a year and you want me to wait even longer."

"One week Tre," Mia begged. "One week and I promise we can sit down and talk to him. I just need to get my mind right before we do."

"Alright, one week or I'm done. I'm not playing this time Mia," Tre threatened.

He would never walk away from her like that, but she needed to know just how serious he was.

"Okay, I'm leaving. I'll call you when I get home," Mia said. Tre walked her to his bedroom door and kissed her before she left.

Chapter 17

Von rode around with Lamar riding in his passenger's seat. This was their fourth day looking for Paige's brother Shad, but they still hadn't run into him yet. He'd been talking reckless about Tre and Von wanted to get to the bottom of the situation. Tre was a grown man, but he still didn't appreciate Shad telling people what he was going to do to his son. He understood that he felt some type of way about his daughters getting beat up, but they deserved exactly what they got. Von wanted to pay somebody to get at them a long time ago, and he was happy that Tre had made it happen. Jumping Mia was a huge mistake that Von was sure that they wouldn't make again.

"Let's ride around the school," Lamar suggested. "He plays basketball in the gym sometimes."

Von nodded his head and drove towards the area that Lamar suggested.

"Did I tell you that Tank has been talking to Terri?" Von asked his best friend.

"Nah, you didn't tell me that. What made her decide to start coming around after all these years?"

"She's sick man. She got that shit," Von answered.

.   "What shit?" Lamar questioned with a puzzled look on his face.

"She got aids nigga."

"Damn, that's messed up. She was a fucked up mother, but nobody deserves to go out like that," Lamar shook his head.

"I said the same thing. But she wants Tank to handle all of her funeral arrangements and shit. She's leaving that nigga a nice chunk of change with her insurance policy too. I can tell he's all fucked up about it, but he's trying to play it cool. He talks to Mia and Duke about everything. You know they're like the three stooges," Von joked.

"I already know. But what's up with you and Tanya? Y'all still playing games with each other I see."

"Not really, we're working towards being together, but she wants us to take our time. I'm not trying to rush her, so I'm cool with that. As soon as it becomes official, I'm kicking Cheryl's disgusting ass to the curb," Von promised.

"I don't know what you see in her uppity ass anyway. She's too damn clingy for me," Lamar replied.

"You ain't lying about that and her daughter ain't no better. She be damn near foaming at the mouth when Tank is around. He don't even pay attention to her dizzy ass. She's cool with Rainey, but Mimi can't stand her ass," Von laughed.

"I'm not surprised. Mia is mean just like Moonie. She don't like nobody, but Brandis. She better not fuck with my baby though. She don't look like her mama for nothing. She'll beat her ass all over your house," Lamar remarked.

"I'll keep both of their asses away from my house before I let it go that far. It's not even that serious between Cheryl and me. She's looking for wedding bells, but I'm not the man for her if she's thinking marriage. I'm not even the man for her if she's talking about a serious relationship," Von confessed.

"Pull up around the back and let's see if his truck is out there," Lamar suggested once they pulled up to the gym.

"Isn't that his red truck?" Von asked while pointing out a Dodge Ram to Lamar.

"Yeah, that's it," he confirmed.

Von parked his all-black Lexus GS Hybrid right behind Shad's truck, and got out with Lamar following close behind. Both men walked into the semi-crowded gym and spotted Shad standing off to the side downing a bottle of water. Shad saw them from the corner of his eye, but he pretended not to notice. He knew that he would probably be seeing Von sooner or later, but he wasn't in the mood to deal with Lamar's crazy ass. Lamar always was a loose cannon and the drugs only made things worse.

"What's the deal Shad?" Von asked getting straight to the point. "I heard you have a problem with my son. Is that right?"

"Yeah I have a problem with that lil nigga. He got somebody to jump on my daughters. My baby's hand and wrist is broken because of him. That shit was foul Von," Shad replied.

"Nah, what's foul is the fact that them ugly bitches jumped on my baby the night before. They got it just how they gave it up. If you have a problem with that you can see me about it," Lamar clarified.

"My daughters didn't jump Mia. They said it was a one-on-one fight," Shad replied.

"And you believed that shit? They can't even handle my girl one on one. They could barely handle her together," Lamar yelled.

"All of that is irrelevant right now. I'm not feeling some of the shit that you've been telling people about what you're going to do to my son. That shit is for lil boys and we're grown ass men. You and I are around the same age, so you should know that I'm not gon' sit by and let you take it there with him. Your daughters jumped Mia and they got jumped in return. All's well that ends well," Von shrugged.

"We can take it to the streets if you still feel some kind of way," Lamar pointed out.

Shad looked at him and nodded his head in understanding. Lamar was the craziest dope fiend that he'd ever met. He could never understand how he was a known user, but still demanded respect like he earned it. Back in the day he did, but those days were long gone. Still, his name rang bells in the streets like he never fell off. Shad didn't mind busting his guns, but some battles just weren't worth fighting. He knew when to back down and this was one of those times.

"We're good," Shad replied in defeat.

He really wasn't afraid of Von, but he did respect him. Von handled things in a different way than Lamar. He wasn't opposed to sitting down having a man-to-man talk, unlike his boy.

"That's good to know. You be cool," Von said giving him dap.

Lamar turned and walked away without uttering another word. He and Von had accomplished what they came to do and all was well at the moment.

"Now how are we going to deal with our other problem?" Lamar asked.

"What other problem?"

"What you mean what other problem? I'm talking about that nigga, Ro. That nigga is telling

244

people that Tank is a dead man walking. I don't take too kindly to people threatening my family," Lamar responded angrily.

"Ro is all mouth. If he really wanted to do something, he's had months to do it. He's a showoff and Tank embarrassed him when he beat his ass in front of his boys," Von said dismissively.

"I still don't put nothing past that nigga. Maybe he hasn't had the time to make good on his threats, but that doesn't mean that he won't. You know how we used to do it back in the day. You make a nigga think it's all good long enough for them to let their guard down."

"I still don't think Ro is going to be a problem. Like I said, he's all bark with no bite. I've known him long enough to know that he ain't about that life."

"Alright, but don't say I didn't warn you. These lil nigga are out here trying to prove a point, but if you're good with it then so am I," Lamar said letting the subject go for now.

He really wasn't all right with it, but he decided not to push the issue. Tank was like a son to him and he loved him as much as he did Mia. Ro was talking about taking his life over a fight, and that didn't sit too well with him. Von might not be worried about it, but Lamar was going to keep his eyes and ears to the streets at all times. If Ro made one stupid move, he was going to be a distant memory.

***

"Brandis," Mia yelled while waving her friend over. "What took you so long?"

She'd been standing in front of the school for the past ten minutes waiting for her to come out.

"That evil bitch did not want to let us out of the class until we wrote down our homework. My hair is soaking wet with sweat," Brandis complained.

The school day had barely gotten started when a car hit the pole out front and caused all of the power in the area to go out. It was a little after ten that morning when the announcement came that they were being dismissed for the day. It was a Friday, so Mia and everybody else were excited to have an early start to their weekend.

"I'm hot and sweaty too. I need to go shower and change before we go anywhere else," Mia replied.

"That's cool with me. A shower is just what I need. I have to wash my hair too," Brandis said as they got into Mia's car.

"Okay, just come to my house when you're done. We can figure out something to do then," Mia suggested.

"Oh no heifer, don't try to be slick. You have to go by Von's house. You know what today is. Y'all are supposed to be making that move and telling Von what's up," Brandis laughed.

"I am going by Von's house, but not until later on tonight. You know I never go over there this early. I'm usually in school around this time anyway. Tre doesn't even wake up this early."

"Stop trying to stall Mia. You need to just get it over with early and stop stressing yourself out. You know Tre will wake up for you if you call him."

"I know, but I'll just wait until I get over there later on. I need to calm myself down a little more."

"I understand honey. I'll be over here as soon as I'm done," Brandis said, right as they pulled up to their apartments.

She got out and walked to her building while Mia disappeared into hers. As soon as Mia opened the door, her smiled brightened when she saw who was sitting on the sofa.

"Hey Mitch," Mia beamed.

He had on a pair of sweat pants and socks, but he didn't have on a shirt or shoes.

"What's up my girl? It's about time I get to see you. You're never home when I come over here," Mitch said giving her a hug.

Mia sat down next to him just as Moonie entered the living room wearing nothing, but a t-shirt and underwear. Mia always suspected that the two of them were still messing around, but she wasn't sure. After seeing them both half dressed, she knew for a fact that something was going on. All of the kids were in school, so Mitch couldn't say that he came over for them. This was probably the time that they usually hooked up since they would have the house all to themselves.

"Y'all had a half day?" Moonie asked her.

"No, the power went out and they let us go early," Mia replied.

"I heard Jabari got you riding nice, huh?" Mitch asked.

"Yeah," Mia replied with a slight smile.

She was always uncomfortable when people asked her about her car, mainly because the story was so unbelievable. Jabari couldn't afford to buy her a car, when he and Tiara needed a second vehicle themselves. Jabari always fell out laughing when somebody mentioned him buying Mia a car, and that made the lie seem even worse when he did it.

"We're about to go get something to eat Mia, you're welcome to come if you want to," Mitch offered.

"I'm good, but thank you. I'm going to take a shower. It was so hot in those classrooms."

"I know you're probably going by Von, so make sure you lock up before you leave," Moonie said right before she walked into her bedroom.

"Okay, see you later Mitch," Mia said before she disappeared into her bedroom.

After rummaging through her drawer for something comfortable to wear, Mia took a nice long shower and tried to steady her nerves as best as she could. She was not at all ready to let Von know about her and Tre being together, but she knew that it had to be done. She understood how Tre felt. She wouldn't like it if her man kept her a secret for over a year either, especially if he claimed to love her so much. As much as she hated to disappoint Von she knew that what they were about to tell him probably would.

"Hey Duke," Mia said answering the phone for her God brother.

"Hey sis, I need a favor," Duke replied.

"Okay. What's up?"

"Can you pick me up from home and take me to Von's house? I left my bike there last night and I need to pick it up. Tank took me home in his car because we got caught in the rain. I left my bike in Von's garage."

"Okay, just let me get dressed and I'll be on my way," Mia responded before hanging up.

She didn't plan on going to Von's house so early, but she would make an exception for Duke. He was always going out of his way for everyone else, so she didn't mind doing the same for him. Since she would be inside of Von's house for the rest of the day, Mia threw on her colorful leggings with a high-low shirt and a pair of tennis shoes. She was about to call Brandis and tell her what was up, right when the doorbell started ringing. She grabbed her phone and answered the door and found Brandis standing on the other side.

"I was just going to call you," Mia told her friend. "I have to pick Duke up. He needs to get his bike from Von's house."

"I know, I'm the one that told him to call you," Brandis laughed.

"You make me sick," Mia laughed with her. "You just want to be nosey."

"And you know it," Brandis replied.

"Let me grab my purse and I'll be ready," Mia said running down the hall to her room.

Ten minutes later, she and Brandis were pulling up in front of Tanya's house. Brandis called Duke and told him to come outside. Another few minutes passed before he came out and locked the door behind him. He opened the passenger's door and pulled Brandis out, so that she could ride in the back seat with him. Mia smiled at how cute they were together. She never imagined them being together before, but they made the perfect couple.

"Y'all want to catch a movie or something later on?" Duke asked them.

"Mia and Tank might be punished after Von finds out what's going on," Brandis joked.

"Mia ain't telling Von shit. I hope you don't believe that," Duke laughed.

"She doesn't have a choice. Tank ain't playing that with her ass this time," Brandis said.

"Okay, y'all gon' stop talking like I'm not sitting right here," Mia chuckled. "And we are talking to Von today and Tre is not making me do it. I just feel like it's about that time to put everything out in the open."

"We'll see," Duke replied dismissively.

Mia stopped and filled her car up and they were on their way to Von's house soon after. Just like she expected, her nerves were starting to get the best of her. The butterflies in her stomach were working overtime. She was kind of hoping that Von wasn't home, but when she pulled up and saw Cheryl's car parked out front, she knew that he was. Von's car must have been in the garage because Cheryl was parked directly behind Tank.

"I'm not saying shit as long as she's here. I don't want her nosey ass all up in my business," Mia frowned referring to Cheryl being there.

"I'm going to get my bike and take it back home. Y'all just call me so we can hook up tonight," Duke replied. "Get the garage opener for me Mia."

They all got out of the car and walked up to Von's front door. Mia used her key and went inside, with Duke and Brandis following right behind her. She went straight to the kitchen where Von kept the garage opener and handed it to Duke. She and Brandis were about to walk down the hall to the spare bedroom when she heard voices coming from one of the other rooms. She thought it was Von and Cheryl talking, so being nosy was Mia's number one objective. Duke laughed when Mia and Brandis stopped and tried to listen at Von's door. He was about to say something, until Mia put her finger to her lip telling him to be quiet. Obviously, they couldn't make out what was being said because they started walking to their destination once again. Just as they were about to go into the spare room, Tre's bedroom door opened and he walked out. Tre was shocked to see Mia and the rest of the crew standing there looking at him, especially since he didn't hear them come in. Mia couldn't help but smile at him, and admire his tall, muscular, tattooed frame. He had on his baby blue basketball shorts with no shirt, and a pair of black socks on his feet. She was about to say something to him until another voice spoke up before she could.

"Are you sure that you're going to call me later Tank? You always say you are, but you never do," a familiar female's voice was heard coming from behind Tre.

Mia's heart shattered into a million pieces and her smile quickly vanished, when she saw London's smiling face emerge from the bedroom right behind him.

Stay Tuned For Part 2.
Coming Soon…

55226935R00156